The Trident's Trap

(Published in Tamil as Athimedu)

Punnaivanam SANKAR

Contetns

Contetns

Chapter 1

Athimedu

Athimedu was a quaint residential spot nestled in a picturesque hilly region. The area was characterized by an expansive view of hills and slopes, with tea gardens blanketing the hillsides in lush greenery. The homes in this residential community were positioned on a small hillock next to a mountain pass, set in a tranquil natural setting. The hillock rises three feet above the road. Each house was a small concrete structure, occupying six hundred square feet, and they were scattered irregularly on the hillock, set back from the road's edge towards the slope of the valley behind.

The spaces between the houses were abundant with greenery and vines. The walkways leading to the houses commenced as a single path along the road's ridge and divided into trails reaching every dwelling. The slope near the homes and the entire opposite hillside was covered with tea plantations, surrounding the residential section with a lush green backdrop. The inhabitants of these houses were the tea estate supervisors and the managers from the tea processing factory situated some distance away. The houses where the tea pickers lived were positioned just below the hill's edge. These were small, terraced homes with asbestos roofs, suitable for only two occupants.

The asphalt road laid three feet below the edge of Athimedu, on one side, linked a town situated atop the hill. On the opposite side, it connected to Kondarapatti, a small village inhabited by hill dwellers. The road split just two kilometres before reaching Kondarapatti, with the diverging path veering to the right and descending to an embankment area at the foot of the hill. A dam was constructed across the river to retain water flowing through the valley at the mountain's base. Additionally, a power station was present to produce small-scale hydroelectric power using the stored water.

Housing for the officials and employees tasked with operating and maintaining the hydroelectric power station was situated on the slope just above the dam. The paved road leading from the dam to the town, approximately twenty kilometres away, was created for the workers in the dam vicinity and the residents of the nearby hills. A bus runs along this dam road once each morning and evening. Besides these buses, traffic on the mountain road included vehicles of officials who occasionally visited the dam. The well-known Jeep of the forest officials was also a common sight. Apart from these, the locals had no other means of transport to and from the hill town.

Walking in the area was deemed hazardous. After 5 pm, only forest department officials were allowed to use the mountain pass, prohibiting all other traffic. This restriction was due to the movement of wildlife, particularly elephants, along the hillside paths. Elephant herds frequently traversed a road section spanning two kilometres from where the embankment road met the tarred road. Besides the disruption caused by elephants, no other dangerous wildlife was reported in the vicinity. This part of the road was marked as unsafe, with warning signs erected along the roadside.

After getting through the hazardous section of the road, there was an absence of animal disruptions. Monkeys were the sole animals visible in some areas. Continuing along the road toward the hill town, there was a complete lack of animal activity. Only humans and their homes were visible. Further upwards, the Athimedu bus stop was positioned right between the hill town above and the dam area below.

From the small stone steps located at the bus stop on the roadside, one could view the entire Athimedu residential area. Positioned approximately forty feet from these steps was Raghavan's home. The walkway to the house began at the road riser, continued to the asbestos shed situated in front of the house, and then veered to the side leading to the back of the residence.

Beneath the shed's roof on the left side, there was a cement seat, while a two-wheeled vehicle covered with an old saree was positioned on the right. The main entrance to the house was shut. The backyard, a bit larger than the house itself, was entirely carpeted with grass, reaching a height of two inches. At the heart of the backyard, a fig tree, having been growing for over fifty years, extended its branches across the whole area. Raghavan stood on the grassy surface, leaning on a crutch under the fig tree's shade.

Standing at six feet tall, his sturdy build required the aid of a crutch for support in maintaining an upright position. His right hand gripped a small handle that extended vertically just beneath the crutch's ring. While the crutch and his right foot were securely grounded, his left foot barely grazed the ground without being fully planted. This condition was not present from birth; rather, it was the result of a recent accident that necessitated the crutch. Without it, he would struggle to balance his legs, maintain a proper posture, and walk without stumbling.

It had only been a few weeks since Raghavan started living alone. Shortly after he arrived, he developed the habit of lingering in the backyard for long periods. He enjoyed the delightful natural view in front of him the nearby hillocks, the more distant hills, the densely grown trees on top, the mountain peaks visible against the sky in the far distance, and the expansive sky above him.

It was noon during the monsoon season. Dark clouds traversed the sky, suggesting the possibility of rain at any moment. Occasionally, sunlight pierced through the clouds, creating patches of brightness and streaks of shade on the grassy field beneath the tree branches. Raghavan was deeply moved by the picturesque natural landscape unfurling before him and the soft, refreshing breeze enveloping him.

The slopes of the hills before him were covered with tea plants. The pathways for human movement between the tea plants were clearly marked as intersecting lines. Between the slope descending from the edge where Raghavan stood and the opposing slope, deep in the valley, the dam's water had overflowed into a large lake. To the right, in the distance, the section of the river that supplies the lake meanders like a white band and vanishes behind the mountains. The valley lake never dries up because the river flows year-round.

Raghavan glanced to his left, realizing he had been standing and admiring the unmatched artwork before his eyes for a considerable duration. He sensed that his legs might be feeling slightly uncomfortable. He desired to take a short break under the fig tree.

The thick central trunk of the fig tree, eight feet tall, looked mangled yet exuded a rustic allure. From where it branched, it divided into a mix of thick and thin bands, creating numerous folds and grooves. These bands detached from the trunk two feet above the ground, weaving around the tree, and vanished into the soil. Raghavan selected a spot on the trunk's natural grid for sitting, though it was an effortful task. He extended his legs and released his right hand from the crutch, setting it on the trunk. Leaning fully, he rested his back and head against the trunk, closing his eyes. The gentle, cool breeze soon lured Raghavan into a deep slumber.

In his dream, a team of about ten to fifteen individuals ventured into the forest. Each person was equipped with an electric saw for cutting down trees and climbing ropes. The group split up to focus on cutting the large, mature trees. They wrapped the rope around their waists and secured it to the tree trunk, ensuring it was easier to climb. An electric chainsaw was suspended from a ring around their waists. As they climbed, they cleared away small branches hindering their ascent with a scythe attached to their opposite side.

Upon reaching the area where the branches diverged at the top, they positioned themselves to effectively cut the branches. Then, they detached the electric saw from their waist and began sawing the branches.

Once the individuals ascended the trees, the birds residing in those trees shrieked and departed, sensing impending danger. Uttering puzzled sounds, they began to circle the trees. Numerous birds that exited the trees flapped their wings and soared away from the area, indicating they were only temporary dwellers in those trees.

After leaving the felled trees, some birds went to nearby trees to rest. Those perched birds were restless, flying close to the trees being chopped down and then returning to neighbouring trees. They moved from tree to tree in agitation, creating a commotion with their loud cries and filling the forest with their screeching. Their nests, containing eggs, chicks, or young birds, might have remained in the cut trees. Flying frantically and crying, the birds did not know how to protect them. The cacophony of birds and the noise of numerous trees being cut simultaneously made the forest a sorrowful place. Meanwhile, the woodcutters focused on their task, indifferent to the bird's cries and noise.

Branches were severed from the trees and began to tumble to the ground. Observing this, the birds raised their cries and flew around the area with a chaotic noise, fluttering erratically without assistance. Two of these birds, in their flight, vigorously orbited a tree. They flew close to the tree's branches, attempting to impede the woodcutter's actions. Furthermore, they made efforts to hit him with their wings and peck him with their beaks but pulled back in fear at the man's movements at the last instant. Repeatedly, they circled the tree without surrendering.

Amid the chaos of cutting the tree branches, the faint cries of three tiny chicks in a nest became inaudible. Only the parent birds circling the branch might have noticed their distressing calls. By then, three-quarters of the top of the branch had been severed and began to slip downward. The woodcutter drove the saw into the branch's base and started cutting the remaining section. In a matter of seconds, the branch was detached from the tree. It fell to the ground, shuddered slightly, and came to a rest.

The two birds, which had been flying nearby, suddenly descended vertically towards the ground with a loud screech on the fallen branch. The screeching sound woke Raghavan from his sleep. As soon as he opened his eyes, two parrots cried out 'kee... kee... kee... kee...' in front of him and swept through the yard with the noise 'virr...' 'virr...' instantly. The parrots passed by him within moments. They were two parrots that had separated from a flock flying from behind the distant hills. Both parrots flew rapidly as though they were in a race, changing positions to the right and left as they moved through the backyard.

Was it the brief flutter of the parrots he heard that roused him? Or was his sleep disturbed by the 'kee... kee...' sounds of the parrots? Or perhaps it was the cry of the helpless birds in his dream that disrupted it? He was uncertain. Letting go of his dream, he glanced up at the sky towards the parrots, suspecting that the two parrots flying by like arrows had awakened him.

In the distance, he observed the parrot flock moving across the sky like a cluster of dots. The two parrots that had flown in front of him might have merged with the group. Soon, the cluster blended into the sky and vanished from his sight.

Chapter 2

Raghavan

Raghavan checked the time on his watch. It was already after noon. Realizing it was time to prepare lunch, he crossed his legs and rose from the tree stump. Using his crutch, he made his way across the grass, opened the back door, and stepped into the house.

The house was small, comprising only three rooms, and was somewhat sparse in terms of furnishings. The kitchen was located to the left of the entrance from the backyard. On a scale of one to ten, the kitchen shamelessly boasts a one for its lack of cookware, left exactly as his mother abandoned it years ago. His bedroom was situated on the right side of the hallway that extended straight from the back door past the kitchen. A dining table was positioned in the area next to the bedroom wall in the hallway.

The font hall stretched approximately ten feet long, matching the house's width. On the left side of the hall stood a table and a chair. Resting on the table were several account books, a pen, a pencil, and a ruler, all utilized by his father. His father would sit there to manage the account matters concerning the tea plantation workers. On the right side of the hall, a small heap of packages was stacked in the corner, all belonging to Manikandan, a local vendor.

In the bedroom, a bed was oriented from east to west. On the eastern wall, facing the bed, hung a glass window covering three-fourths of the wall, complete with a curtain. The bathroom was located to the window's left. The room was small and furnished with basic features.

From the porch, one could see vehicles and people traveling on the paved road through the mountain pass. Across the road, the hill's slope was blanketed with wild vines and dense trees.

Located about ten feet to the right of Athimedu's stairs was a small shop owned by Manikandan. The shop's opening hours varied daily, but typically he conducted his business from 8 AM to 5 PM. While it wasn't a large-scale operation, Manikandan's shop played an important role in the local community. For several years, it provided residents with necessities such as rice, dal, oil, other groceries, and personal care items. He took great satisfaction in his work.

Some years back, he extended his offerings to clients by setting up a 'tea' boiler outside the shop and began serving 'tea'. The bus driver and conductor on that route during mornings and evenings became regular patrons of Manikandan. Occasionally, some passengers alighted to visit his establishment as well. Besides that, he operated a small business catering to travellers using two-wheelers, cars, jeeps, and vans. Supplies for the shop were loaded from the town onto the bus and unloaded at the Athimedu stop. Manikandan would keep the unloaded items in Raghavan's house hall and move the required supplies to the shop from there.

Following his lunch, Raghavan walked into his bedroom. He leaned back on the bed, set aside his crutch, stretched out his legs, and gazed at the scene outside the window opposite. The fig tree and the hills beyond it caught his attention. While lying on the bed, he could see only a portion of the trunk with its branching section. Most often, it was the mountain landscape that captivated him. Occasionally, the slight changes in the scenery caused by shifting clouds, at times by swirling snow gusts, and rarely by birds passing through would catch him by surprise.

The morning's scattered clouds had concealed much of the sky by noon. In the distant horizon, the mountain ridges were entirely veiled by clouds, while the mountain ranges in front appeared faintly beneath a layer of snow. Despite the snow covering the nearby hillocks and the tea gardens on the slopes, the faint visibility of the landscape provided him with a visual delight and a tranquil mind. That silence was short-lived. His gaze shifted from the far view outside the window, and he settled back in the room to relax his stretched legs.

Upon noticing his injured leg and the crutch, the incident that forced him back home vividly replayed in his thoughts. The jolt from this recollection reverberated through his body, resulting in a mild tremble before subsiding. Raghavan began reflecting on past events from a few months ago, prompted by the quivering that awakened those memories. He found it hard to grasp that he survived while his friend Senthil Kumar, from his hometown, along with a few others, perished instantly in a bomb explosion. Upon his voluntary retirement from the military, he recalled the day he came back to Athimedu.

The morning light in Athimedu was uniformly spread out. Two women were standing in front of Manikandan's small shop to buy something. Manikandan was arranging items on the board in front of the shop and filled the boiler with water to prepare 'tea.' Upon hearing a bus approaching from afar, he instinctively stepped out of the shop, saw the bus arriving, and went back inside to resume his tasks. After some time, the bus halted at the stop. The driver signalled for Manikandan to check the rear of the bus.

While inside the store, Manikandan noticed the signal and glanced back at the bus. A passenger disembarked, and the conductor leaned over, giving a bag to someone below. One bag was passed, then a second, followed by the whistle cue from the conductor for the driver to set off. The bus began to move slowly. From the shop, Manikandan observed two bags placed sequentially on the ground, with Raghavan standing beside them.

The man, unseen for quite some time, suddenly made an appearance. Manikandan observed that Raghavan's usual glow had faded, and he appeared somewhat weary. Manikandan did not comprehend the cause. Overcome with surprise at the unexpected sight, he swiftly exited the shop and dashed across the road to Raghavan. Midway, Raghavan's state struck him, prompting him to approach and embrace him. As Manikandan began running towards him, Raghavan anticipated his intentions, and upon being hugged, he applied extra pressure on the crutch to maintain his balance. Upon noticing Raghavan's situation, he released his clasp and touched the crutch, inquiring, "Why is this?"

Raghavan stared sternly at Manikandan, grasping his shoulder with his left hand and urging him forward. Manikandan picked up Raghavan's two bags and slowly crossed the road to the tea shop, where Raghavan sat down on the wooden bench.

Raghavan and Manikandan attended the same school and were classmates until the tenth grade. Manikandan could not pursue his education further as he had to take over his father's business.

While enjoying the tea that Manikandan had brought, Raghavan succinctly shared the tale of how and why he has come back to reside in Athimedu permanently. Even though the story concluded suddenly, Manikandan pondered over it in silence for a while. After some time, he took him home, reassuring him with the words, "Alright, Raghava... you don't need to worry about a thing... we are here to support you." As they entered the house, Raghavan was astonished to find it unchanged from how he had left it. Sensing his thoughts, Manikandan explained, "Indeed, Raghava, no one visits here but me and my wife. I use this hall for storing my shopping items. My wife comes by regularly to clean the house."

After conversing with him for some time, Manikandan headed to his store. All at once, the quietness that pervaded the house wrapped around him. Raghavan perceived that this silence and its enduring tranquillity seemed unending. Consequently, Raghavan embarked on living alone in that house indefinitely.

While stretched out on the bed, Raghavan's thoughts drifted from recent events to the view outside, where the scene beyond the window gave him a fresh sense of hope.

Chapter 3

Tea pickers' Homes

Encouraged by the hope he felt the previous evening, he slept through the night and awakened the next morning feeling rejuvenated. The light began stretching behind the far-off mountain peaks on the horizon, indicating the arrival of sunrise. The tea plantations covering the nearby hillsides appeared a dim dark green, owing to the faint light. The clusters of trees that stretched skyward on the mountain peaks seemed unmoving, akin to elements of a painting. Birds occasionally flying through the valley made him aware that the scenery before him was not a mere painting. In addition, the diverse sounds from birds perched on the top branches of the fig tree offered a backdrop of music to the scenery.

The sun climbed above the mountain peaks, casting its fresh light. The rising sun was obscured by the main trunk of the fig tree, revealing only a portion of its edge on the tree's left. Sunlight scattered from that edge, illuminating the area with a flash, giving the impression of the sun emerging from the fig tree's edge. This sight faded away in a few minutes. Raghavan rose from bed, leaving his crutch, and moved slowly to the window to gaze at the view outside, his face pressed to the glass.

As he gazed at the tree, the sprawling branches filled his view, and the sky's blue hue peeked through the leaves, filling him with a sense of elation. Clusters of figs appeared on the branches separating just above the trunk. From small pods to fully matured fruits, the figs clung and dangled in bunches throughout the tree. The fruits were narrow at their base, expanding like a cone, and the top of this cone-like form converged into a small depression, resembling a spinning top. The ripe ones displayed a lovely purple, others were reddish orange, while the pods were a fresh green, and some were a mixture of hues. Across the tree, thousands of figs were spread out, either individually or in groups, on every branch.

While observing the tree and its fruits, Raghavan noticed a slight movement in one of the highest branches. Up there, a squirrel leapt from the top of the tree, circled a branch, and quickly descended to the tree's base as if fleeing from some danger. At that moment, another squirrel came down the same branch, making a 'ceek... ceek...' sound just a foot behind the first squirrel's path, chasing with equal speed and reaching the lower part of the tree. The initial squirrel then jumped to a different branch, circled it, and climbed back to the tree's top. The pursuing squirrel mirrored these actions, following it to the top. The first squirrel leapt to yet another branch and began descending once more, with the trailing squirrel in close pursuit. The leaping and chasing of the squirrels continued.

A few minutes passed before Raghavan understood that the squirrels were merely playing. He ceased observing them and shifted his focus to the right, toward the window. He could see the backyard behind the house, followed by rows of tea pickers' homes. Adjacent to this, the tea plantation's slope stretched out briefly, culminating in a flat terrain densely populated with wild vegetation and shrubs. Beyond this, the tea plantations sprawled beneath the expansive blue sky on the horizon.

Amid the vast tea fields, he noticed the well-known tea processing facility. This was the workplace of his father. He had frequently visited it, accompanied by his father. He observed the trail threading through the line of tea workers' residences on the side, cutting through the thick brush to arrive at the tea factory in the distance. Raghavan's father had prohibited using that path, always permitting only the paved route. Hence, he paid complete attention to that side path for the first time. Raghavan's eyes shifted from keeping watch in the backyard, descending the incline to the lake at the valley's base.

The grassy field extended from the bottom of the slope to the lake's edge. Across the expansive lake, the same grassy expanse reached up to the opposite hillside. The slope on the other side of the valley was also blanketed with tea plantations. Raghavan observed these natural vistas with keen interest as if he was seeing them anew. Despite having lived there since childhood, he felt that he had never fully appreciated the joy that nature provided him. He began to think about going closer to immerse himself in the places he observed. With this intention, he promptly finished his work and prepared to head out.

Raghavan retrieved his military uniform from the box and, as he glanced at it, recalled that it was meant for specific events. Yet, he contemplated wearing it another time. He removed the insignia from the cap and donned the entire uniform. Dressed in his military attire, with the cap adjusted to his right ear, he stood at the doorway, feeling ready to step out at any moment. For a moment, a sense of hesitation enveloped him.

Leaving the shed, he paused at the junction of the paths and noticed the route to the tea mill on his left. A question he had never thought of before entered his mind. Why had his father forbidden him from taking that path? Moreover, he had personally tried to avoid using that route to the mill whenever possible…!

With that question lingering, his eyes shifted to the road stretching towards the dam. A motorcycle zipped toward the embankment. Then, his attention moved to Manikandan's shop on the right side. The shop was open, with a few customers gathered in front. Raghavan initially took two steps toward it, but abruptly reconsidered, turning left to follow the path leading to the tea plantation instead.

As his curiosity about why the path was off-limits grew, he wondered if walking down it might reveal the reason. Encouraged by this thought, he set off with determination and arrived at the settlement of the tea plantation workers. There, the path broadened until the row of houses ended and then became narrow again as it led into the tea slope. Fifteen houses stood side by side, tightly packed without any gaps between the small dwellings. The men and women had all departed to work in the tea garden.

Towards the end of the lane, a group of boys were engaged in play. Raghavan began to make his way across the terraced road. When he was halfway, a tiny item rolled towards him and struck his shoe. He halted and glanced down to identify the object that had bumped his foot.

Stooping to retrieve the rounded item at his feet, he recognized it as a paper ball. A newspaper sheet had been crumpled, rolled into a sphere, and encased with thin thread to almost resemble a ball shape. However, due to its slightly heavier weight than mere paper, Raghavan surmised that a small stone might have been embedded inside the paper ball for added weight.

Meanwhile, a boy who had run to retrieve the ball approached Raghavan and halted when he was five feet away. The boy shifted uncomfortably where he stood, intimidated by Raghavan's attire and hesitant to speak since Raghavan held the ball. As Raghavan reached out to hand over the paper ball, the boy acted. He lifted his right hand slightly above his chin and saluted Raghavan, stating, "He threw it." The boy then glanced back at the children who were standing further away.

Raghavan was slightly taken aback to see a boy with torn trousers and a poorly buttoned shirt salute him. He gave the paper ball in his left hand to the boy, who then turned and ran back to join the other boys without waiting for Raghavan to free his right arm from the crutch to return the salute.

Feeling somewhat let down, Raghavan grasped the crutch once more and began to traverse the path anew. The children who were playing there paused their games and approached him, encircling him on either side as they began to trail behind. Paying no attention to the boys, Raghavan proceeded along the route past the houses and made his way into the tea garden slope.

As the boys attempted to trail him, a female voice interrupted, "Hey... don't go there...! Come and play...". Heeding her words, the boys promptly turned around and headed to the play area. This occurrence caused Raghavan to pause and glance back towards the voice.

In front of the house second to last, a girl who appeared to be the same age as the boys sat on the steps with a baby beside her. It seemed she oversaw looking after the neighbouring infant and had influence over the boys. She appeared unaware of Raghavan as he walked past. The boys, under the persuasion of the young girl they were playing with, began splitting into groups to resume their game. Though taken aback, Raghavan kept walking, dismissing the matter from his mind.

Chapter 4

Stone Stage

At ten in the morning, the sun was mild enough for Raghavan as he strolled leisurely through the dense tea plants lining the path. The sky had a few clouds. Raghavan felt elated watching the top tea leaves bend and tilt... tilt... swaying evenly with the wind as the gentle breeze came from the southwest.

With enthusiasm spurred by the weather and surroundings, he advanced until halted by a bush-covered plain just below the slope of tea plants. The bushy expanse, roughly the size of a basketball court, was dense with wild vegetation, morphing it into a thicket. From his position, a path, two feet wide, cut directly through the thicket and continued into the tea garden opposite. At the path's end to the right, about ten feet distant, a peepal tree towered high, casting shadows over the shrubbery with its branches. Abruptly, the sight of the sprawling bush area dissolved Raghavan's excitement, replaced swiftly by a profound silence that enveloped him.

Losing himself in the tranquil ambience and taking a brief stroll down the path, he was halted by the sight of a stone stage visible on the right. At that moment, he found himself in the centre of the zone. It was there that the mystical atmosphere of the area started to reveal itself to Raghavan.

He stood there, surveying the surroundings briefly. Outside the bushland, sunlight bathed everything, enhancing the beauty of the valley. Far off, tea picking was happening in some spots. However, within the bush, it appeared to him that the peepal tree was casting a shadow, dimming the area.

The leaves of the gigantic peepal tree extended their long tips in the occasional southwest breeze, swaying back and forth, producing a rustling noise. The rustling of the peepal and the wind's 'hiss' joined together, interrupting the area's silence and giving the deserted place a mystical feeling, which made him shiver a little. Considering the option to leave right away, he reconsidered and opted to rest on the stone stage for a moment, weary from the lengthy walk. Even though he planned to depart later, he approached the stone stage with hesitation.

The stone platform, which measured ten feet by ten feet, was located approximately fifteen feet from the peepal tree. There were steps along the path leading up to the two feet high stone platform. Peepal tree fruits were strewn across the stone platform and the nearby areas. The small, dark blue fruit bulbs would burst open when they fell from the tree, revealing their insides and drawing ants and small wasps to swarm over the entire area.

Amid the fruit splashes on the stone platform, a foot-tall Trident was embedded in the centre of the platform. It had three sharp spikes at the end of a pole, with two spikes bent towards the centre. Curiously, a fresh cigar was placed on the platform before the Trident, appearing to be an offering to it. The stone stage and the Trident rooted in it evoked a sense of unease for Raghavan. Nevertheless, feeling weary, Raghavan used his left hand to clean the edges of the stone platform, set aside his crutch, and took a seat on the stage.

He settled down and spotted the peepal tree on the right. Raghavan felt relieved to see the thickly grown tree standing about ten feet tall trunk, with its branches spreading widely over the years; the numerous leaves on the branches were swaying with the wind, with patches of blue sky visible beyond. He leaned back, arms stretched behind him, his face turned upward, eyes closed. The peepal tree's shade and the gentle breeze provided relief from the discomfort of traversing the mountain slope, and Raghavan remained there, unaware of the time passing by.

He remained seated, oblivious to the small ants that were traversing his hands from behind. The moment he heard gentle footsteps nearby; he lifted his head with closed eyes and gradually opened them. As his eyes adjusted, the figure before him sent an electric jolt through his nerves, resulting in a full-body tremble. In a split second, Raghavan stumbled off the stone platform, faltering and tumbling to the side on the steps of the stone stage.

Raghavan saw the figure once again before him in his collapsed state. Despite his wide-open eyes, the grotesque elderly figure in front of him sent a slight chill through him. Observing Raghavan's shocked fall onto the stone steps, the old man stepped forward to assist. However, Raghavan soon realized that the figure was indeed a human being. He motioned with his right hand to halt the old man, wobbled a bit, and took a seat on the stone stage's steps, only to stand up immediately. Once upright, he retrieved his crutch lying nearby, steadied it in his grasp, and began to closely inspect the elderly man who had caused him to stagger.

The elderly man, who had surprised him, remained standing before him with the same unnerving expression, even though Raghavan regarded him serenely. The man, around five feet high, had a gaunt face with recessed cheeks. Apart from a section of his forehead, his small nose, and his deep-set eyes, the upper part of his face was shrouded in thick, dirty brown hair. The hair above his forehead and eyebrows jutted out slightly, enhancing the depth of his eyes.

The elderly man, with a mane of shaggy hair and penetrating eyes, was fixing his gaze intently on Raghavan. Raghavan noticed the striking blood-red saffron mark on his forehead, encircled by an inch-wide band, adding to the grotesque appearance of his face. The man's mouth was concealed within a dense mass of hair blending with his moustache and beard. He was bare-chested, exposing a ribcage over a sunken abdomen, with arms where the skin clung tightly to the bones. A black dhoti draped from his waist down to his ankles.

In his hands, which were thick like bones and covered in leather, the elderly man strangely held some objects. Various coloured torn fabrics were wrapped around his right arm, from just below the elbow down to the wrist. The fabric ends protruded from the wrap and splayed out over the cloth beam. On his left arm, he adorned a collection of bangles in multiple colours, extending from his wrist to the elbow.

Raghavan noticed peculiar items visible on his legs. There was a yellow cord tied around his right ankle. The frail old man had a tarnished silver anklet on his left ankle. Despite his bravery in facing numerous perils in the army, Raghavan found himself somewhat disturbed by the old man's grotesque look.

The old man was gazing intently at Raghavan, not bothering to give him a full once-over. The old man's eyes sparkled with recognition upon seeing Raghavan and lit up with joy. His face was filled with the happiness of finally seeing someone he had been anticipating for a long time. Raghavan observed the apparent transformations on the old man's face but couldn't comprehend the reason behind them. In a state of confusion due to past events, Raghavan was bewildered by the changes he saw and stood there, unsure of what action to take.

He lifted his left hand and gestured towards his house as though he intended to speak, yet no words emerged. Observing this, the elderly man lifted his skeletal hand, halting Raghavan from voicing anything, saying gently, "You are Soman's grandson, aren't you…!" His voice, mingling with the breeze, aimed to verify that he had identified Raghavan.

Raghavan felt somewhat reassured when he noticed that the old man's presence wasn't evident in his voice. The old man's voice resembled the muted sound of sawing a piece of paper with a dull blade. He called Raghavan 'Soman', which took a moment for Raghavan to recognize as referring to his grandfather, 'Somanathan'. The old man perceived Raghavan's silence as a response to his query and went on with his light, gentle voice, "You... have come...! good... very good..." he expressed.

Without waiting for Raghavan's response, he abruptly turned and began heading towards the tea garden. After covering a short distance, the old man came back and yelled, "I will visit you... soon" before continuing his way.

Astonished by the unexpected occurrence, Raghavan remained still, watching the path the elderly man took. By that time, the older gentleman had made it to the far end of the bush path. Despite his years, Raghavan was amazed to see the old man walk steadily without tripping or wobbling.

Although the old man and Raghavan had not met before, their initial encounter unexpectedly left Raghavan confused. Yet, when the old man departed after mentioning Raghavan's grandfather's name, it dawned on Raghavan that perhaps there was a connection between his family and the old man.

Uncertain of his next move, he looked over where the old man had gone. By that time, the old man had already entered the tea garden slope and was out of view. Raghavan turned back to see the Trident lodged in the stone stage with a fresh cigar in front. He considered heading towards the factory in the direction the old man had taken. However, he dismissed the idea and retraced his steps homeward.

Returning to the tea slope via the path he initially used, the distressing incidents he experienced in the bush slowly diminished, replaced by the serene ambiance of the tea garden. Raghavan had drawn near to the workers' residences.

The kids were playing in that area. Upon arriving, he observed that the girl remained seated on the doorstep. The infant was absent. The girl was jotting down something with a notebook on her lap. Raghavan approached slowly and took position at the entrance of the house.

The young girl, engrossed in her task, paused her writing and looked up when she sensed someone at her doorway. Raghavan gazed at the girl, who lifted her head and asked, "Could I have some water to drink...?" Without uttering a word, the girl tucked the small pencil from her right hand into the notebook resting on her lap, shut the notebook, set it on the step, and promptly rose to go inside the house to get water. The infant was sleeping in the cradle within. Shortly after she departed, she returned with a pitcher full of water and handed it to Raghavan.

Exhausted and thirsty from his lengthy travels, he drank the water she provided and handed the empty pitcher back to her. Feeling a bit better after quenching his thirst, he got ready to settle on the doorstep, planning to take a short rest there. At that moment, he noticed the notebook the girl had left on the top step.

The cover opened a little, revealing the lines in the top right corner of the page that caught him off guard. In the corner of the notebook's first page, which was worn and creased, he read "D. Raghavan, IX 'B', History" vertically...

It was his own handwriting, his notebook… he was confused. Raghavan, more intrigued, grabbed the notebook and settled on the second step.

By that time, the girl had come back in and stood leaning against the doorway. Raghavan only turned his head to show the notebook to the girl, asking, "What do you think?" The young girl understood and replied, "Father gave it…". Raghavan then turned his attention away from her, flipping through the notebook. As he turned the pages, he saw the history notes he had written in ninth grade, with words like 'Panipat,' 'Ibrahim Lodi,' and 'Chandragupta Maurya' in his handwriting. The page-turning stopped where the pencil was resting.

On the blank page at the end of the latest history lesson, the girl had sketched a drawing. It resembled a pigeon soaring through the air. As Raghavan glanced back at her, the girl descended from above, stood before him, and exclaimed with excitement, "I made it myself." She then retrieved a small piece of paper attached to the notebook and offered it to him. This piece of paper had a printed picture of the pigeon she had drawn.

However, Raghavan noticed a discrepancy. The picture she drew did not have a leaf. Realizing it might have been a mistake, he nonchalantly quizzed her, "Why is there no leaf in the picture you have drawn?". She retorted, "The pigeon is on its way to pick the leaf…". This took Raghavan by surprise. Her reply was unexpected, and it naturally flowed from her rather than being a planned explanation for the omission Raghavan mentioned in her drawing. It showed her ability to think on her feet. Added to that, her innocent expression attested to her genuine sincerity of the answer. Unsure of how to respond, and with a light tinge of defeat, Raghavan rose quietly.

Surprised by the little girl's response without speaking, Raghavan glanced at the boys playing nearby. They were all looking for something among the tea bushes, possibly their paper ball. He turned to the girl, who was watching him intently, and asked, "What is your name?" She replied, "Poonkuzhali." Following that Raghavan asked, "your father?" In response, she pointed towards Raghavan's house and said, "The petty shop…, he is there."

Mildly surprised, he asked, "Who…! Is it Manikandan?" The child nodded in affirmation. Raghavan felt a sharp pang in his heart, saddened by the realization that he knew nothing about Manikandan's family. He then asked her, "Well, where is your mother?" She pointed towards the tea factory in the distance, saying, "She works there, and she'll return in the evening." Additionally, she mentioned, "Next week, I will join her at work."

Raghavan recently discovered that the girl was the daughter of his good friend. Feeling embarrassed, he decided not to linger any more. He informed the child, "Alright, I'm on my way" and departed for home. He gave her the notebook and started towards his house. The young girl remained standing, observing him leave with the notebook in her grasp.

Chapter 5

Fig Tree

That afternoon, Raghavan was lounging on his bed, reflecting on the morning's happenings. The first to come to mind was the grouchy old man. Initially, he felt a pang of fear at the sudden sight of the man's silhouette, but recalling the man's appearance quickly dispelled that fear. He considered meeting the old man once more to learn about the connection with his family. It occurred to him that asking Manikandan about the old man might provide some leads.

He discovered that Manikandan had named his daughter Poonkuzhali, which he found to be a lovely name. She was attentive and caring towards the children and the infant in the household. 'She is a graceful young woman with both knowledge and aptitude' he evaluated. Raghavan felt a bond with Poonkuzhali due to her being Manikandan's daughter, leading him to feel compelled to do something for her.

Her nonchalant response to his question on her drawing about the leaf and the bird, 'it's going to pick the leaf,' echoed in his thoughts. He perceived that her reply carried a certain intelligence. Could a child with such intellect be permitted to work in a tea factory? He was seriously considering finding a way to prevent it and ensure she attended school. He planned on discussing it with Manikandan and his spouse. Raghavan concluded when he recognized that the day's events seemed to point toward Manikandan. He resolved to meet with Manikandan first thing the following morning. A feeling of moral clarity settled over him as he contemplated the meeting, clearing away his doubts. Rising from the bed, he slowly headed to the backyard to unwind.

The evening sun's shadow stretched across the backyard from Raghavan's house. Fig leaves blanketed the ground, with some figs poking through here and there. Small groups of clouds dotted the sky. The wind was chilly. He meandered slowly and settled on the twisted roots that resembled the lap of a fig tree, leaning against it. Soon, he fell asleep as dreams took hold of him.

Raghavan found himself all alone in a thick forest. As he looked around, he understood he was in a deserted wilderness area. Out of the blue, a hunter appeared from a distance, aiming an arrow at him. Raghavan was frozen with fear. He couldn't escape from the hunter. His legs felt anchored to the ground, unable to move. He wished to raise his arms and scream, "Oh…! No." However, his hands wouldn't respond, and no words emerged from his lips.

The hunter released the arrow, which sliced through the air in the direction of Raghavan. In a split second, the arrow shot through his chest and emerged from his back. As soon as he sensed the arrow had gone through his chest, he quickly turned around. The arrow exited his back and struck a Trident fixed on the ground. Upon impact, the arrow vanished, evaporating into nothingness. As he observed, the shimmering silver Trident also disappeared, dissolving into the air. Raghavan quickly turned forward, realizing the hunter was no longer visible. Instinctively touching his chest, he found no evidence of an arrow's penetration. Subsequently, all the scenes dissipated into a slight blur within the expansive smoke zone.

Simultaneously, an additional scene manifested in the hazy area. The images were indistinct as well. A female officer was striding quickly down the veranda, her gaze intense and piercing. Behind her, a few officers were trailing, clutching files. Several police officers were both running and walking nearby. The woman arrived at the entrance to the officer's conference room. At the room's entrance, two officers saluted her and opened the door. However, the lady officer paused momentarily, neither saluting back nor stepping inside. She glanced at Raghavan, offering him a gentle 'salute' accompanied by a smile, before entering the room. Despite being a haze to Raghavan, the lady officer's face seemed quite recognizable. Without the opportunity to see her face once more, those scenes vanished, and the smoky area faded away as well.

A new scene emerged in the same location, steeped in a frightening ambiance. A forest of thorny bushes extended before Raghavan, with the absence of trees stretching to the horizon. The area was filled entirely by wild plants and thorny shrubs. In the distance, Raghavan noticed a man pulling something along. Intrigued, he promptly pursued the man to scrutinize more closely.

The moment he saw the scene, he was stunned, and his steps faltered. A remarkable incident was unfolding there. Raghavan felt crushed upon noticing that the man was pulling a human skeleton. With one hand, the man grasped the skeleton's wrists and pulled it across the sandy ground surrounded by vegetation.

As the skeleton's skull wobbled from side to side with the drag, its legs spread apart and dangled from the pelvis, continuing to draw lines in the sand in arcs along the pull's direction. Then the left foot bone got caught in a nearby bush. The man stopped dragging the skeleton and attempted to clear the blockage. To address this, the person who returned bent down, shook the bone in another direction, and jiggled it back and forth to quickly free it from the bush. Once the obstruction was cleared, something detached from the ankle strap suddenly shot up and flew towards Raghavan's forehead, who was following behind.

The object launched from the skeleton and struck Raghavan's forehead with force. His sleep was interrupted as he exited his dream state. Upon waking, he discovered that he had been napping beneath the fig tree in the backyard. The occurrence in the dream had him disoriented. The frightening images caused him to shudder slightly. Consequently, his body started to shake. The chilly wind outside intensified his shivering. He remained seated, reflecting on the dream's events.

Why was that arrow launched towards him? Who was the person it targeted? What was his connection to the person? What could be the significance of the arrow that passed through him harmlessly and struck the glowing Trident behind before vanishing instantly? Raghavan pondered these questions repeatedly and found himself unable to determine any explanations.

The unanswered dream was followed by a nightmare that started to bewilder him. What was the thing that splattered and struck his forehead? He was pondering over this when his right hand instinctively rubbed his forehead. No matter how hard he tried, he couldn't recall the face of the person who had pulled the skeleton. When the man attempted to release the skeleton's legs from the shrubs, Raghavan recalled noticing a scar on his head as he leaned down. It was pointless. That dream was also incomprehensible to him.

Likewise, he had no explanation for the second dream that occurred in between the other two. The face of the female officer in Raghavan's dream appeared recognizable to him, as though he had encountered it somewhere before. Yet, who could it be? His mind grappled with making even a rough guess.

Yet, in a part of his mind, he sensed that the female officer's face slightly resembled the girl he had encountered earlier that morning. 'How is that possible?' Seeing a young girl, he met in the morning as a high-ranking officer in his dream...! 'What could this signify?' These thoughts drew Raghavan's attention back to Manikandan's daughter Poonkuzhali's circumstances.

Raghavan found it hard to forget the assistance Manikandan provided. Having left home after college, Raghavan could only visit infrequently. In his absences, Manikandan took care of his father and managed other family responsibilities on behalf of Raghavan. Notably, when Raghavan's father passed away unexpectedly, it was Manikandan who stepped in to conduct the funeral rites in Raghavan's absence.

Raghavan's heart was filled with guilt as he realized he knew nothing about Manikandan's family, whom he regarded as a brother. 'When did Manikandan tie the knot?' He couldn't recall. 'What is his spouse's name?' He had no idea. 'He has a daughter.' That, too, was news to him. Embarrassment overwhelmed him. During a brief encounter with the girl, Raghavan perceived that Poonkuzhali was sensible and smart.

He felt disheartened at the thought that the bright child would soon be working in the tea factory. 'Why has Manikandan chosen to have the child work at such a young age? What could the child possibly earn to contribute? What benefit does this have? Is poverty the cause, or is there another reason?' In the middle of these reflections, Raghavan suddenly had an idea. 'Regardless of Manikandan's reasons for not enrolling Poonkuzhali in school, what if she could be given the chance to study?' Raghavan resolved to speak with Manikandan and his wife the following day to seek their approval for sending Poonkuzhali to school.

Rising with resolve, Raghavan sensed that he had discovered purpose in his retired life. As though endorsing his choice, a fig leaf dropped onto his head and landed on the ground. Swiftly followed by another leaf, the fig tree commenced releasing its foliage upon him as though providing a leafy shower. Within moments, branches throughout the tree began losing their leaves, crafting an illusion of leaves raining in his backyard.

The shower of leaves stirred Raghavan's emotions as he stood beneath the fig tree with his crutch, sending Goosebumps across his skin. A few moments later, the leaf shower ceased, and Raghavan gazed up at the motionless branches and leaves of the fig tree, which resembled a still painting. The leaf fall, occurring in the absence of wind or branch movement, appeared miraculous to him. He embraced the event as a benediction from the fig tree for his choice regarding Poonkuzhali.

Chapter 6

Manikandan

The following morning, Raghavan arose early, completed his tasks, and prepared to visit Manikandan. He left home dressed in regular clothes instead of his military attire to go to Manikandan's shop, which was open. On glancing at Manikandan's house on the left, he was taken aback by what he saw.

The elderly man he encountered at the stone stage the prior day was sitting on the steps of the last house, and Poonkuzhali was observed handing something to him. He felt an urgent need to meet with Manikandan and resolved to inquire about the old man as well. He chose to head towards the shop, intentionally ignoring the situation unfolding there.

Descending to the paved road and positioning himself in front of the shop, Manikandan enthusiastically invited Raghavan to join him and had him take a seat on the wooden bench provided. Subsequently, Manikandan began allocating the goods in small baskets from within the shop onto a board protruding from the establishment.

The shop was empty, and while attending to his tasks, he remarked, "I meant to tell you to drop by whenever you find the time." Then he added, "Is there a reason you've come by so early?" Manikandan inquired with a grin as he gazed at Raghavan. Without delay, Raghavan replied, "I need to discuss something with you, and I value your opinion on the matter."

"It looks like you have plenty to discuss, well... Anyway, hang here for a bit, and I'll wrap up my breakfast and return. Chitra needs to head to the factory. I also need to have a conversation with you." He implied he could chat at ease. Raghavan mentally noted that 'Chitra' is Manikandan's wife's name."

After some time, Manikandan completed the task of organizing and showcasing the items and mentioned, "Alright, I'll return shortly," as he began to exit the shop. Raghavan then questioned him, "What happens if a customer comes to purchase something while you're away?" Manikandan responded, "There's nothing you need to do; they'll manage it on their own." He folded up his dhoti and proceeded to the rear of the shop.

Raghavan, left by himself outside the shop, examined his surroundings. Beside the bench where he was seated, a boiler heated water for tea, with a stove burning gently underneath. Inside the store, numerous items were packed in small packages. A wooden chair, meant for Manikandan, stood in the middle with a compact weighing machine positioned ahead of it. On the shop's shelves, various goods, suitable for purchasing and selling in small quantities, were neatly arranged.

A small two-foot display in front of the store featured mostly vegetables and fruits. At that moment, two women arrived to make purchases. The newcomers glanced at

Raghavan. Disregarding him, one of them confidently entered the shop and began gathering items for both. To his astonishment, he kept watching their actions. He recalled what Manikandan had mentioned before leaving the shop. The woman who had entered the store began handing the items over to the other woman standing outside. Afterward, the woman inside the store also collected the items she needed.

Both determined the cost of the goods they took based on the price tags attached to the individual bundles or cardboard boxes. They opened the wooden drawer beneath the weighing machine, placed the money inside, and retrieved the necessary change. Raghavan observed that Manikandan had written the price for each item on small pieces of paper, which he placed in the respective baskets or attached to the boxes. Most of the product prices were quoted for quantities not exceeding a hundred grams. Upon concluding their transactions, the women glanced at Raghavan once more before leaving the store, engaged in conversation. Once the women vanished from Raghavan's view, Manikandan came back to the shop.

He immediately entered the shop and turned up the heat on the boiler stove for brewing tea. Shortly after, he served two steaming cups of tea in glass tumblers, gave one to Raghavan, and sat down next to him.

After silently finishing their tea, he put the empty glasses by the boiler and sat beside Raghavan, saying, "Alright, let's hear it. You mentioned there's something we need to discuss!" Then Raghavan took Manikandan by surprise with an unexpected gesture. Holding Manikandan's hands, Raghavan, with a remorseful expression, pleaded, "Mani...! I'm sorry, please forgive me."

Manikandan, taken aback by the unexpected event, exclaimed, "What... Raghava! Why are you doing this? What did I do to you?" Looking at him, Raghavan responded, "Mani, you've been like a brother to me and have done a lot for my family. Yet, I knew nothing about yours," he expressed with regret.

Manikandan responded, "Oh... Raghava! What I did is insignificant. You and your father have done so much for me. Don't you realize that? We studied together until the 10th grade. Even though I didn't do well academically, you and your father pushed me to complete my tenth grade. Then, I unexpectedly lost my father and felt alone. Your father treated me like a second son. He was the one who found a bride for me. Look at your house, which I'm still residing in. I ride your father's 'bike' as if it were mine. Thinking about all this brings tears to my eyes. Yet, you are seeking forgiveness..." he said, tears welling up in his eyes.

Raghavan, without altering his expression, remarked, "Even as you mention it, you're assisting me greatly." During this exchange, an older man walking along the dam road veered towards the shop. As the pair's conversation was disrupted, the man requested beedi and a matchbox from Manikandan. Manikandan went inside the shop, accepted the money from him, placed it in the cash drawer, handed him the requested beedi and matchbox, and returned to sit beside Raghavan.

Raghavan observed the actions of the elderly man. The individual who purchased the beedi pack disposed of the stamp paper that encased it appropriately and selected one beedi. He used his thumb and forefinger to grasp it without applying pressure. He then placed the flattened end of the beedi in his mouth.

He removed a match from the box and struck it to light it. He cupped his hands around the torch to shield it from extinguishing as he lit the beedi. He inhaled deeply through the glowing tip of the beedi a couple of times. Once satisfied that it was burning properly, he inhaled deeply and exhaled the smoke upwards.

He prepared for another draw, relishing the thin trail of beedi smoke that escaped his puckered lips, spreading and fading into the air. A sense of relief crossed his face, as though the concerns in his mind had been swept away by the beedi smoke. Thanks to the elder's intervention, Raghavan and Manikandan had altered their previous condition and regained their usual peace of mind.

Raghavan began straight away. "Mani…! Yesterday, I was near your home and spotted your daughter Poonkuzhali. I then found out that you're planning to send her to work at the tea factory next week. Why not enrol her in school instead? This has been bothering me since then." Manikandan stared at Raghavan for several minutes without responding, then abruptly stood up and went into the shop.

He drew out the cash drawer, opened it, and presented it to Raghavan just as it was. Raghavan stared at him, puzzled. He remarked, "See this! Fifteen rupees and sixty paise, that's our earnings up to now. If it reaches fifty rupees by evening, I'm fortunate. Chitra's salary is also low. We can't afford to educate Poonkuzhali. Plus, she's a girl. That's why..." he trailed off.

Raghavan gazed at Manikandan with pity and remarked, "Mani, you're speaking without realizing your daughter's worth. Fortunately, I'm here. We will enrol Poonkuzhali in school next week," he stated with determination.

"Raghava! How is this possible? How do you keep everything going?" Upon seeing him, Raghavan responded, "Don't be concerned about it any longer, I will handle everything. You don't need to think about the schooling costs." Realizing their discussion had concluded, Raghavan got to his feet. Before heading home, Raghavan mentioned, "I'll visit your house this evening and speak to your wife to get her approval as well." Without waiting for Manikandan's response, Raghavan made his way towards his home."

Raghavan arrived at Manikandan's house in the evening before nightfall as per his plans. Realizing there was no seating available indoors for a conversation, he settled on the doorstep. Inside, the mother and daughter were busy with cooking tasks.

Poonkuzhali told her mother that Raghavan had arrived and taken a seat. Chitra promptly came to the door and said, "Welcome, brother! He'll be here shortly," referring to Manikandan's expected arrival, then returned to resume the cooking she had interrupted. Poonkuzhali occasionally glanced back at him, offering friendly smiles.

The boys observed on the opposite side earlier today were energetically playing despite the chilly wind. Manikandan was spotted walking away from the shop in the distance. He sat down beside Raghavan on the house steps and remarked, "Raghava! You're here? Let me check if there's anything for you to eat."

Chitra served hot, boiled tapioca on small plates to both individuals and instructed, "Please eat this first." Raghavan accepted it and told Chitra, "I need to have a conversation with you." She answered with "Alright..." and remained seated where she was.

Raghavan was seemingly well-known to Manikandan's wife, who began to call him Brother in a rightful manner. This made Raghavan realize that while he was unfamiliar with Chitra, she already knew him. Just as he thought it was the right moment to discuss his purpose for visiting, Chitra addressed Raghavan, saying, "Brother, please refer to me as 'Chitra'. I've been acquainted with you since before my marriage. We are truly delighted to have you at our home today." Chitra expressed her joy.

Raghavan gave an approving nod and called over Poonkuzhali, who was behind Chitra. As she approached, he seated her between himself and Manikandan, then turned to Chitra and announced, "I am here to discuss Poonkuzhali." Chitra watched Raghavan with curiosity. He went on, "I'm here to prevent you from sending Poonkuzhali to the tea factory for work. The child must attend school," he insisted firmly.

Upon hearing this, Poonkuzhali, positioned between Manikandan and Raghavan, swiftly leaned towards Raghavan, took hold of his hands, and placed her head in his palms. The way the child acted clearly indicated her wish to attend school.

Observing this, Chitra remarked, "Brother! our situation...". Raghavan interrupted her and added, "It's not right to make a school-aged child work. Moreover, the government assists such children with some educational needs. You don't have to be concerned about Poonkuzhali. I will handle everything concerning her education; it's my duty," he stated firmly before standing up as if the conversation was complete.

Before leaving the house, Raghavan said, "In the morning, I'll head to the government school in town with Poonkuzhali, where I studied. Have the child ready by eight o'clock." Turning to Manikandan, he asked, "Is the 'bike' at home in good condition?" Without waiting for a response, Raghavan returned home. Manikandan nodded silently, as if answering the question affirmatively. They watched Raghavan depart, with Chitra feeling amazed and Poonkuzhali smiling contentedly.

At eight o'clock the following morning, Chitra waited at Raghavan's doorstep with Poonkuzhali. Raghavan instructed them to head to Manikandan's shop. He started the motorcycle by the door, descended the hill, and halted in front of the shop, instructing Poonkuzhali to hop on. Manikandan emerged from the shop, gently placed his hand on Poonkuzhali's head as she sat on the bike, and advised, "Listen to Uncle Raghavan and follow his instructions." "Okay... bye," she cheerfully bid farewell to her parents and set off towards the town.

Chapter 7

Poonkuzhali

Towards the close of the rainy season, occasional showers occurred. Even though the sky was overcast that day, it didn't rain. Raghavan encountered no obstacles enrolling Poonkuzhali in school, even though admissions for the academic year had closed two months prior. Poonkuzhali was already six years old. The headmaster questioned her and was very impressed by Poonkuzhali's responses. He promptly escorted her to the first-grade classroom and allowed her to enter after discussing with the class teacher. Returning to Raghavan, he instructed him to collect her in the afternoon and informed that the child's parents should visit the next day to finalize the application process.

Raghavan exited the school. The school and its nearby area were places he knew very well. He wondered about how he would pass the time until noon. He detached the crutch from the bike and gradually made his way to the street.

Water from the rain pooled along the edges of the street. He began to walk along the roadside, observing each shop. The store he sought was near the school. It stocked all necessary items for schoolchildren. Raghavan purchased all the supplies required for a first-grade child there. He left the belongings at the shop, mentioning he would return to pick them up in two hours, and headed back to the paved road.

Raghavan found himself instinctively walking to the Government Public Library located across the street. He was well acquainted with every part of the library. After wandering through the library at a leisurely pace, he arrived at the common section, entered it, and started browsing aimlessly through each bookshelf. On the fourth shelf, a book caught his eye, prompting him to pick it up and leaf through its pages. The book, titled 'The Fig Tree', contained detailed information about fig trees, complete with illustrations and photos. Intrigued, he took the book to a nearby table and sat down to read. The fifty-page book offered him an abundance of surprising facts. Despite having a fig tree near his home, he realized he knew little about it.

A fact in the book that caught his attention was that the fig tree was regarded as sacred. Its history spans back thousands of years and was associated with deities. Even though the book mentioned there was no proof for these claims, when Raghavan read this information, he trembled briefly as he recalled the incident that occurred beneath the fig tree.

It was already past noon when he completed the book. Recalling that 'school' would soon end, he shut the book and exited the library. He returned to the stationery shop to collect the items he had picked up for Poonkuzhali. Additionally, he purchased two plastic balls for the kids in the tea garden and a play box with picture puzzles to amuse Poonkuzhali, then proceeded to school.

A few minutes later, the 'school' was dismissed, and the children began to emerge. Students from across all classes poured out and hurried toward their waiting parents who were ready to take them home, and they also looked for the vehicles arranged for their transport. Poonkuzhali spotted Raghavan amidst the crowd and dashed over to stand before him. Her face lit up with an indescribable joy. After taking her back to Athimedu, Raghavan dropped the child off at Manikandan's shop and mentioned he would return home that evening.

That evening, the same group that had gathered the previous day met once more at Manikandan's doorstep. Raghavan arrived there slightly ahead of time. He handed out the plastic balls he had purchased to the boys and encouraged them to play. Additionally, he provided them with a somewhat larger ball and suggested they use it for playing football. The boys were excited to have a genuine ball and equally delighted by the new game Raghavan introduced to them. They began playing football in teams of five, using two lines to represent the goalposts.

Upon noticing this, Raghavan proceeded to sit on the doorstep of Manikandan's house. He was served boiled tapioca. As soon as he settled down, Poonkuzhali joined him and took a seat next to him. She eagerly recounted the morning class lessons one by one, clearly delighted. Chitra, seemingly in agreement, also joined them near the doorstep and remarked, "Brother! Kuzhali really enjoyed 'school.' She's been talking about it ever since she returned."

Raghavan handed over the morning's purchases for Poonkuzhali along with the bag. As she received it, her eyes widened in astonishment, almost as if witnessing a miracle. With enthusiasm, she extracted each item individually, showed them to Raghavan, and started organizing them next to her. From the bag, she retrieved and stacked: a board, a class 1 textbook, and two notebooks.

She removed a pencil case, opened it, and was astonished to find a row of pencils inside. She counted them individually and exclaimed to Raghavan, "Ten!", her eyes wide with excitement.

Raghavan stepped in and pulled a pencil from it, then gave it to her. As she took the pencil in her hand, she gazed at it for a few moments and placed it against her cheek, inclining her head a bit as if resting on it. This was the first time she had ever held a whole pencil in her hands.

Poonkuzhali carefully returned all the items to the bag and entered the house. Both Raghavan and Chitra noticed her purpose for going inside, although Raghavan couldn't see anything from his spot. Smiling softly, Chitra looked back at Raghavan and mentioned, "She has positioned her bag before the deities."

After leaving her book bag, Poonkuzhali returned and sat beside Raghavan, holding his right hand and resting against it. Although Raghavan hadn't done anything extraordinary, his gesture left a significant impression on the girl. Noticing that she couldn't openly express her enthusiasm for studying, Raghavan gently touched her head with his left hand and softly patted her, signalling 'I'm here with you from now on'. During this poignant moment, Manikandan arrived and joined them.

Chitra stood up, went inside to get a bowl of boiled tapioca for him, and then resumed her seat.

"See, Mani, your child's interest in her studies," and "How could you think of sending her to work in a tea factory?" Manikandan glanced at Raghavan and nodded, an expression of helplessness on his face. Behind him, Chitra was overjoyed, feeling confident that her daughter had a promising future.

Raghavan handed some cash to Manikandan, instructing, "Tomorrow, all three of you must visit the school to finalize the application procedures. Additionally, purchase Kuzhali's uniforms." He then briefly outlined the process for sending Poonkuzhali to school starting Monday.

In the morning, when Manikandan departs for the shop, he is responsible for taking Kuzhali and sending her with the other children headed to school from Athimedu, on the bus arriving from the dam. In the evening, Manikandan needs to collect Poonkuzhali, who departs from the bus heading back to the dam. Typically, Chitra oversees preparing her for school in the morning. There's no need to pack lunch for her as she receives a midday meal at school. Everyone agreed to this plan. Poonkuzhali was enrolled in school at the appropriate time. With this resolution, Raghavan went home feeling at ease.

The following morning, Manikandan, Chitra, and Poonkuzhali arrived at his house. Informing him that they were going to complete the task he had discussed with them the previous day, Poonkuzhali waved 'Bye' to Raghavan and joyfully ran after her parents as they headed toward the road. Raghavan watched until all three boarded the bus, and just as he was about to head back to the house, his eyes shifted toward Manikandan's home, where he noticed the elderly man standing at the entrance.

Feeling disheartened to find Manikandan's house locked, the elderly man settled on the doorstep. Nearby, women from the surrounding homes were organizing garments and hanging them on vines. They paid no attention to the old man, as it appeared to be a usual event for him to visit there each morning.

However, he was confused about what he was acquiring there. Choosing to inquire, Raghavan entered the house, picked up his crutch, and returned to the door, avoiding eye contact with the old man. The old man was gone. Aware that he couldn't locate him, Raghavan went back inside.

After completing his tasks and settling down to relax, he heard approaching footsteps at the door. The trio who had left for school earlier in the day were entering the house. Poonkuzhali, the child, hurried past the others with a bag in her hand and handed it to Raghavan. Inside, her school uniform could be seen.

Upon rising and seeing Manikandan, he remarked to Raghavan, "Yes, it's already prepared." Curious about the task's outcome, Raghavan inquired, and Manikandan replied, "We returned immediately after successfully completing everything." "Alright… how did you manage to arrive so soon? There's currently no bus!" questioned Raghavan. In response, Manikandan explained, "A friend of mine gave us a ride," mentioning that the friend's name was 'Uthamaraj', a Forest officer responsible for patrolling the dam and the nearby hill area, 'Kondarapatti'.

Manikandan wrapped up by mentioning that the patrol officer noticed them in the market street and asked about them, then gave them a ride in his vehicle before departing. After conversing for a bit, they went back home. As he was leaving, Manikandan called out, "Raghava…! Uthamaraj is very pleased that Poonkuzhali has started her education thanks to your efforts." He added, "Uthamaraj mentioned he wants to meet you the next time he is in the area."

Raghavan was unaware that meeting Uthamaraj would soon develop into a strong friendship, one that would bring about various unexpected and risky adventures. He ended his thoughts with Manikandan by saying, "Alright, let's find out."

Chapter 8

Malaimayan

Over the following days, Raghavan, who kept himself indoors, frequently watched Poonkuzhali as she left for school in the morning and returned in the evening. He also ensured that she was attending school with joy. One morning, recalling the old man, he came to Manikandan's shop at ten o'clock, with a resolve to find out more about him.

While attending to customers and occasionally conversing with Raghavan, Manikandan began discussing their school days. It was the same school they both attended and as they delved into memories, they both became enthusiastic, eagerly recalling each event. Their conversation momentarily touched on academics before quickly transitioning to sports. Manikandan began reminiscing about the football games they often played during their school days.

Although Raghavan did not say anything in return, he was listening to him with great interest. "Raghava... do you remember...! football, we played right? When we were at school, I used to just say 'goodball', 'goodball' instead of football." I realized that it was football, later. Raghavan remembered the game of 'Goodball' they had played, and his eyes widened reminiscing the scenes.

The events of the Goodball game ran in his mind, 'Manikandan used to bring the ball. As soon as he entered the field, the ball used to be forcibly snatched from him and placed in the middle of the field. The ball used to be in sight for a few more minutes. Everyone in the class used to stand in two groups as if bound by some invisible truth. Self-made goalkeepers also used to emerge. All these were short-lived. Important to the game, someone used to become the referee. Normally a wounded fellow. The whistle given by the teacher used to be handed over to him with confidence. Considering it as an honour he would start blowing it erratically. It used to be very difficult to stop him, he had no idea when to use it and funnily enough, no one on the field seemed to care about it. Everyone was busy focusing on the ball gallivanting across the field.'

Among the 'referee's' numerous whistles, a random one would unexpectedly get the game started. The game began when someone in the middle of the field kicked the ball aimlessly. Everyone stationed on both sides of the field, including the goalie, ran toward the ball like arrows. But by then, the ball had already been surrounded by nearby players, receiving their random kicks. Runners from a distance also rushed in, encircling the group and kicking with the sole intention of somehow contacting the ball. Everyone on the field worked together as a single team.

The group cantered around the ball moved slowly in a particular direction, like a cyclonic storm. The storm-like formation shifted to the side, leaving the ball outside the boundary line while stopping inside the field, bound by the rules. When someone threw the ball back into the field, the storm-like formation reformed around it and moved in the opposite direction toward the other boundary. At no point did it move toward the goalpost. The goalies were not there either; both had joined the group surrounding the ball. The referee, too, was caught in the crowd, moving along while blowing his whistle incessantly. No one paid attention to him. The game continued until the end of the period, and then the ball was handed over to Manikandan. It was his responsibility to submit it back.

Raghavan was unable to hide his smile emerged out of the Goodball game he witnessed in his mind. Manikandan looked at Raghavan, who smiled at such a humorous game of 'Goodball' and asked, "What?". Raghavan told him briefly what he saw in his mind. After spending a few minutes reminiscing about those old memories, Manikandan's face suddenly changed and with mixed feelings of disappointment and helplessness, "Raghava! I always brought the ball. And it was me who used to promptly return it as well. We have been playing for so many days, but my feet never touched the ball even once" Manikandan said pitifully to vent his disappointment but with a tinge of laughter.

Raghavan, already struggling to hold back his laughter due to the humour sparked by the 'Goodball' game, erupted into laughter when he saw Manikandan's expression as he claimed the ball hadn't hit his foot even once. Observing this, Manikandan joined in the laughter. The pair of friends were amused by thoughts of the 'Goodball' game until the distant noise of a motorbike interrupted their laughter, drawing their attention.

Several seconds after they noticed, the sound of the bike gradually subsided and stopped in front of the shop on the road. A man got off his bike, took off his helmet, stuck it on the bike's rearview mirror, and came to the shop. As soon as the bike stopped, Manikandan said to Raghavan in a low voice, "Raghava... I told you about Uthamaraj... It's him." Raghavan nodded his head in understanding. By then, Uthamaraj came in front of the shop and sat next to Raghavan, looking at him.

Manikandan started making 'tea' for him. While preparing the tea, he introduced Raghavan to Uthamaraj, "Sir... He is the one who got Poonkuzhali admitted into the school". Uthamaraj extended his hand to Raghavan, and both shook hands. Raghavan said to him, "Sir! Mani told me about you," Uthamaraj replied "Likewise about you too..." By then, Manikandan had brought tea for both and sat beside them with a cup in his hand for himself as well.

Manikandan slowly asked Uthamaraj, "What sir? Is there any news left for today?" Hearing this prompt, without hiding anything, he said, "Yes Mani, a leopard has appeared. I must go now. The rangers have already left" and he got up frantically, saying that he should post people on the watch tower and warn the people. They handed the empty glass to Manikandan and told both, "I am coming", and got down on the bike towards the dam.

Raghavan watched Uthamaraj, following him with his eyes until the noise of his bike faded away. After turning back, Manikandan remarked, "Next to the Dam is a village called 'Kondarapatti' where wild animals frequently wander into human habitation. Leopards, bears, and elephants are often seen, and occasionally tigers." He added, "Sir has been losing sleep for at least ten days now. When he returns, he will share his story with us, and we will listen." With that, he headed back into the shop to attend to the customers.

Raghavan then stood up with the intention of heading home but suddenly recalled the old man. He started inquiring about him from Manikandan, saying, "Mani, I came here to ask about that old man, but I somehow forgot." Manikandan quickly responded, "which old man are you talking about? wait, wait, here I am." and promptly dismissed the customer before coming down from the shop.

"Last week, on one occasion, I noticed that elderly man at your door, and Poonkuzhali was giving him something. Another time, when you were at school, I spotted him again in front of your locked house," Raghavan went on to ask, "Who is that man? What is his connection to you? Why is he wandering around like this?"

"I can't tell everything about him all at once" Manikandan said urgently and started his questions towards Raghavan. "Why are you asking about him?" Have you already met him?" he asked nervously. Raghavan replied calmly, "Yes". Manikandan asked without abating, "Where?" "Beyond your house under that peepal tree", said Raghavan.

After a moment of silence, Manikandan asked, "Did the old man tell anything?" Raghavan replied, "Nothing much... He told me the name of my grandfather and informed me that he would come and meet me later." Raghavan continued, "I do not know how he knows about my family?"

"He knows not only about your family but about all the people in Athimedu. But no one really knows about him fully. Where does he come from…? Where does he go? Everyone here is afraid to see that Malaimayan and stay away." Manikandan said further, "There are only two people who can talk to Malaimayan without fear. They are Poonkuzhali and Chitra. I don't fear him much, but I feel a little disgusted when approaching him".

Looking at Raghavan, who was keenly listening, he started shedding some irrelevant information incoherently, as if he didn't want to talk much. 'That old man had never talked too much to anyone. God comes directly to him and often speaks to him it seems. Soolamuni is his god, who is stationed on the stone stage as a small Trident.' Further, he wondered, "Look… though he is nearing a hundred, how he walks at this age…" and stopped. After a while he himself continued, "But there is no disturbance or harm to anyone due to Malaimayan. Anyway, stay away from him," he finished as if there was nothing to talk about further.

However, things unfolded in a manner completely contrary to his expectations. Despite Raghavan not grasping the entirety of Manikandan's information, it sparked a curiosity in him to further explore Malaimayan. Consequently, within a month, Raghavan found himself needing to meet Malaimayan once more, leading to a certain level of closeness between them.

Raghavan, who rose early that morning and began his work, found that his curiosity about Malaimayan, which had been growing over the past month, had transformed into a burning desire that day. He hastily completed his morning tasks with the aim of meeting Malaimayan to inquire about the facts.

Due to Manikandan's remark that he was not easily approachable, he began his search for Malaimayan without knowing where to start or whom to inquire. Upon reaching the doorway, he was astonished to find Malaimayan seated on the cement slab beneath the home's shed, wearing the familiar expression he had observed under the peepal tree that day.

As Raghavan stepped outside, he gazed at him, appearing as though he had been anticipating this moment, and he smiled. Malaimayan rose and entered the house assertively, gently nudging Raghavan aside. The intruder surveyed the room, approached the daily calendar on the wall, and began tearing off the calendar sheets gradually. With patience, he removed the pages that had been left untouched for months. Upon reaching the present date, he paused and turned to look at Raghavan.

Raghavan was still at the doorway of the house, observing Malaimayan's work when he heard Malaimayan's call. He approached him and saw a calendar page from 1990. The date shown was September 18. Raghavan glanced at Malaimayan's face, puzzled and unsure of what to make of it. Malaimayan indicated the black circle on the calendar page with his index finger.

Understanding its significance, Raghavan slowly uttered, 'New Moon Day.' Malaimayan corrected him by saying 'Mahalaya Amavasya.' He added, 'This was the day we sacrificed Soma.' After stating this, he gestured for Raghavan to join him as he began moving toward the backyard.

Even though the events there bewildered Raghavan, Malaimayan's words captivated him, prompting him to chase after Malaimayan and stand beneath a fig tree. By then, Malaimayan had already moved beyond the fig tree and was positioned at the hill slope's edge.

Raghavan gradually moved to stand close to Malaimayan. Malaimayan pointed his right hand toward the lake nestled at the base of the valley and remarked, "It happened here…. three decades ago." Malaimayan's voice was tinged with sadness and sorrow as he spoke. Raghavan speculated that his grandfather may have drowned in that lake and passed away.

Malaimayan came back silently and stood under the fig tree. He tapped his hand on the tree and leaned against it, then turned to Raghavan and said, "Soman planted this fig tree as a young sapling right here on his wedding day. See how much it has grown now."

Malaimayan took a seat where Raghavan used to sit, under the foot of the tree, observing the large branches sprawling overhead. Positioned on the blanket of fig leaves laid out on the ground in front of Malaimayan, Raghavan looked at him. Malaimayan appeared to merge with the wrinkled tree trunk, and his expression was particularly sombre and grim.

Raghavan observed Malaimayan seated with a look of concern in his eyes, burdened by the weight of memories and a tragic event that occurred thirty years prior. Raghavan started to develop a sense of respect and admiration for Malaimayan, who was preoccupied with thoughts of a person who had passed away three decades ago on this very day. He firmly grasped Malaimayan's hand in a gesture of comfort. Any revulsion that Malaimayan's presence had initially caused vanished from him.

Considering Malaimayan as his kin, Raghavan addressed him, "Grandpa! It appears that past events are troubling you. You seem eager to share something with me. I've grasped parts of what you've mentioned, but not fully. Please tell me everything that you've come to discuss," he requested, bowing to Malaimayan.

After observing Raghavan for a few moments, Malaimayan spoke softly, "Brother Raghava! I have much to share with you; I returned home this morning to convey everything. I can't reveal it all right now. I'll tell you some now and the rest later." He paused to breathe. Raghavan nodded in agreement with Malaimayan's words, "Alright."

Malaimayan shut his eyes and drifted into past recollections. A few minutes later, he opened his eyes and started narrating an eighty-year-old story in his casual tone. Even though Malaimayan couldn't recount the events in a coherent manner, he intermittently closed his eyes, attempting to visualize the old events as scenes and narrate them to some degree.

Raghavan sat earnestly, like a student eager to learn from his teacher. The tale spanned eighty years, and Raghavan started to grasp what had transpired by picturing the events described through Malaimayan's mental imagery as much as he could. Raghavan's eyes widened at the ancient tale.

Chapter 9

Friends

Every day for the past week, a van was seen parked in the town's main area each morning. The individuals arriving in the van recruited workers for the tea plantations in the hills. They informed everyone that accommodation and meals would be provided at no cost. Additionally, they promised a monthly wage for the employees. In the evening, the van transported those who agreed to the offer up to the mountains.

That morning, the van was stationed at the Mariamman temple grounds in the heart of the town as they began their search for workers. Their announcement caught the attention of two orphan boys seated in the temple hall. The promise of free lodging and meals in the announcement particularly appealed to them.

The boys themselves were unsure of how they reached the temple. They had been relying on the temple for several years. For sustenance, the occasional alms of the temple and the morning and evening Amman Prasad were sufficient. Additionally, during special temple days, they would carry torches and flags alongside the palanquin as Amman idol processions down the street. They were paid five paise. This was their income and livelihood. A life without any thought for their future.

The job announcement for the tea estate appeared to be a turning point that captured their interest. Both wandered from street to street with the group who arrived in the van until noon and returned to the temple hall feeling disheartened.

The individuals arriving in the van regarded both as youngsters who were there just for their enjoyment. Typically, those who napped in the temple hall during the afternoon were awakened by the evening chatter of many conversing. The van stationed there was prepared to depart with the individuals who consented to work.

Both left temple the hall and went near the van. Ten or fifteen men and women were sitting inside the van. Some additional people still needed to board. The two of them attempted to enter the vehicle, but the driver prevented them. He had instructions not to transport boys who might be as young as fifteen for work.

The individual responsible for checking the van for everyone reporting to work proceeded and joined the driver. The van began to leave slowly in front of the disappointed boys. Then, as if an idea struck one of them, he chased after the van, not worrying about his friend. As he approached the van, he clung to the iron hook on its side, stepped onto it, and leapt inside. The other boy, observing this, instinctively followed suit to get into the van, and both joined the group inside. The van accelerated towards the hill.

That night, the recruiters discovered the two boys at the foot of the hill where they had been residing. Unsure of what to do with them, they decided to take them along, planning to inform their boss the following day and handle the situation then. Spending the night there, they journeyed uphill the next day and were eventually left at their lodging by the evening.

The following morning, as the two boys were brought to work, they paused for several minutes, mesmerized by the majestic mountains of their new environment. Both witnessed an extraordinary view unlike anything they had experienced in their fifteen years of existence.

Mountains and peaks covered in green stretched as far as the eye could see. In the distance, the horizon seemed to blend seamlessly with the light blue sky. The sun had risen and illuminated the hill's lush greenery. Towering trees were perched on the mountain ridges, while on the hillsides, trees and plants resembled shrubs.

Winter had just begun, and the cold wind made both boys shiver a bit. Twelve months earlier, a man from Europe named Alan Williams purchased a sizeable portion of the mountainous terrain they observed. He arrived six months prior, set up camp, and initiated the transformation of the wooded land to accommodate tea plantations.

Everyone brought in for work was led to an asbestos shed nearby. Inside, Alan Williams was seated prominently in an antique chair. The man, standing at a height of at least six feet, wore a long white shirt with grey pants, and his shirt was neatly tucked in.

Fastened at the waist of the pants, two leather straps extended over his shoulders and down the back, securing his pants at the waist. His head had locks of brown hair that extended beyond the neck and down to the shoulders at the back. Sideburns descended from in front of the ears and merged with the beard covering the chin.

The beard was trimmed to its edges, giving a facelift. The tips of the moustache were curled upwards next to the nose, instilling fear in those who looked at him. Before him stood all the new arrivals in a line.

The two boys were joined last in line. Alan Williams, with a brown moustache and beard covering most of his face, began to examine the workers one by one with his brown eyes. After the short examination, they were placed in suitable jobs.

After the people were given their job assignments, it was time for the boys. Alan Williams was a little stunned to see the boys there. He looked to his assistant, who explained how they had come to be present. Alan asked the boys "what is your name?" to the one standing first. He said, "Somanathan," and pointed to the other behind and said, "he is Mayan."

Alan Williams inquired of the boys, "Did you come ready to work?" Once he received their affirmative response, he accompanied them along with the other servants. Within the next thirty minutes, they arrived at the location where the initial tasks for the tea garden were underway. The variety of activities spread across the hillside was somewhat challenging to comprehend. It was clear that this was their workplace, yet the specifics of their tasks were unclear to them.

Preliminary efforts were underway to transform and clear the slopes of the hillside areas, dense with bushes and trees, into tea plantation slopes. Some people were busy clearing smaller vegetation and bushes, while in certain spots, mature and well grown trees were being felled mercilessly.

The sound of lumbering saws echoed across the valley, pounding the entire region. Alongside this, the noise of trees collapsing lifelessly onto the earth, the sounds generated by cutting the tree branches, and the cries of diverse bird species that had long inhabited those trees. The birds' anguished calls, circled the whole mountain area in their helplessness to stop the felling, unveiled the distressing reality of the forest's destruction.

Soman and Mayan were not affected by the deforestation events. On the contrary, the climate conditions fuelled their enthusiasm. With the same energy, they began their assigned tasks, such as removing small bushes and transporting chopped tree pieces in wheelbarrows. Gradually, they developed an attachment to their work and started enjoying it.

Within a few months, the work to create a tea plantation started with the clearing of forests. Deforested areas were cleared for tea plantations, and tea plants were planted. The maintenance work of the tea plantations already cultivated had also started. Beyond the emerging tea plantations, deforestation also continued as an extension work.

Soman and Mayan were employed in tea plantations. Before long, they impressed everyone around them. Their clear dedication and passion for their tasks caught the attention of Alan Williams, who observed them closely. Gradually, a closeness began to form with Alan Williams.

In just a few years, the area's forests were entirely eradicated to establish tea plantations, transforming the whole hillside into a tea estate. The daily task involved gathering tea leaves from the entire garden. Alan Williams had constructed a tea factory on-site to process the harvested leaves into tea powder.

Located half a kilometre north of the tea factory, Alan Williams commenced constructing a large mansion for himself. The two friends, in their twenties, roamed the tea garden as adults and mainly received jobs in the tea plantations. Alan Williams often took both to the mansion under construction and involved them in the design of a unique hall inside. They both puzzled over the purpose of such a large hall within the enormous mansion.

Soman and Mayan would head to a peepal tree situated at the top of the hillslope for a small business during afternoons when there wasn't any task in the garden or mansion. The peepal tree was located just below the mountain slope's edge. The whole area was dense with brambles and bushes, making it difficult for anyone to access. Finding the peepal tree convenient, they gradually created a single-track path leading to it. When work was relatively easy, they would sit under the peepal tree and smoke beedi there.

That afternoon, the two companions walked through the shrubs and smoked beneath the peepal tree. They had two reasons for choosing that spot: first, it was deserted, and second, it provided a view of the whole hillside and valley area.

Standing at the peepal tree, which acted as the lookout, there was a tea plantation to the right, surrounding areas beside it, and a tea plantation stretching endlessly to the left. Directly ahead lay a lake at the valley's base, framed by the mountain slopes and forests, all within sight.

The mansion was the only thing obscured by the peepal tree and the bushes. The two of them observed the opposite hillside of the valley, inquisitively blowing out smoke. By the lakeside, a team was working. There, preparations for a small boat to traverse the lake were underway. It only remained to watch its construction finished in a month's time.

After preparing the boat, it was possible to reach the opposite shore of the lake. But what lay ahead? To the right, the tea plantation on the slope ended, and on the left side, there was a densely wooded area unsuitable for tea cultivation.

They were informed that the forest region was quite perilous. They understood that wild animals wandered freely and occasionally visited the lake edge to quench their thirst.

Although they had never witnessed dangerous animals approach the water, they had occasionally observed groups of spotted deer moving back and forth. The sight of a boat being prepared on the lake's shore drew their attention, sparking a small wish in their hearts to board the vessel and travel to the other side.

They did not know then that their wish would come true very soon and boating would become part of their lives.

The boat was prepared ahead of schedule and ready to set sail. A test run was scheduled for the week's final day, with one of the boat builders designated to paddle. That morning, Alan Williams brought Soman and Mayan to the lakeside.

Even though the pair were slightly puzzled about why Alan Williams had invited them, they were glad to be with him. Alan Williams's look that day surprised them.

Departing from his typical white and grey attire, he donned a dark blue shirt that extended to full length along with matching pants, secured with a leather belt. Adorned with a hat on his head, clutching a double-barrelled firearm, and a bandolier of bullets draped over his shoulder, he had the appearance of an ideal hunter.

Soman and Mayan were seeing a gun up close for the very first time. Observing their frequent fearful glances at it, Alan Williams reassured them, saying, "No need to worry, we won't be hunting today, but we will from this point onward."

Afterwards, he turned to Mayan and pointed to a man nearby holding an oar, instructing, "He will guide you on how to manoeuvre and row the boat for a week. Then, all three of us must go hunting." He proceeded to sit in the boat, then brought Soman and Mayan onboard. Following them, the rower climbed aboard as well, and the boat slowly made its way into the lake, embarking on its initial voyage.

The friends found the show to be incredible. Mayan was keen on learning how to sail but was hesitant about joining Alan on a hunting trip. Soman felt it was his duty to participate in the hunt with Alan Williams in addition to handling various tasks at the tea plantation.

After the boat arrived at the other side, the trio disembarked and observed the mountainside and the woods for a moment before getting back on the boat. They concluded the day's journey by boating on the lake for some more time.

Mayan was unable to ride a boat and from then on, he started practicing rowing and rowing. Within a week, Mayan had mastered sailing the boat. Alan Williams was happy with that. Mayan used to take Soman and often go around the lake for fun in the boat. Life seemed blissful to them. Apart from working hours, they spent time under the peepal tree and boating.

One day, an extraordinary occurrence awaited those who gathered beneath the tree to smoke beedi as they usually did. The pair of friends contentedly sat under the peepal tree. Soman retrieved the pack of beedi from his pocket and began to separate them. Mayan grabbed a match for his portion, and at that instant, the beedi pack in Soman's hands slipped and dropped to the ground.

The dropped bundle gradually rolled forward, slipping into the dense shrubs ahead, where it vanished. Unable to act, Soman glanced at Mayan, who looked back holding a match, seemingly questioning what had transpired.

To amend his mistake, Soman descended from beneath the tree, approached the bush, crouched, and peered into the shrubbery where the pack had gone in. It was not seen as the bushes were very thick. Persistent in his endeavour, Soman uprooted the small plants from around the bush and discarded them. He then jostled the stems of the slightly larger plants and began to move one by its roots.

Regardless, he intended to find the beedi pack since they were eager to smoke it that day. Quickly, the plant he seized was uprooted and ended up in Soman's hands, though the top part of the plant remained caught in the bush.

Holding onto it tightly, Soman exerted his entire strength to pull it out with his hand. His success motivated him to attempt to remove other plants nearby from the earth. Once he had uprooted each plant, he crouched and investigated the bush to check if the bundle could be seen.

Even after pushing aside a couple of plants, his eyes failed to find what they were seeking. It must have tumbled a bit deeper. Soman, who stood up with a bit of fatigue, began pushing aside the bushes above and peered through the created gap. Inside, he witnessed a startling sight. Soman quickly stepped back twice, as though he had touched a flame. He was drenched in sweat, his body trembling. Observing Soman's confusion and the alarm on his face, Mayan descended from the tree and moved to stand before Soman. Upon witnessing the startling scene within, he immediately leaned against Soman, who was standing behind him.

Chapter 10

Amman Idol

Astonished by something concealed within the thorn bush, the two stood in silence, gazing at one another for several moments. After a brief pause, the group moved to the area where the bushes had parted, collaborating to push them further apart, creating an opening through which they could quietly look inside. What they saw was beyond belief. There lay a square stone stage with a five-foot-tall statue of a goddess, elegantly posed, enshrined at its centre. As they looked more intently, the entire figure of the goddess statue gradually became visible to them.

At the centre of the visible square stone stage, there was a meticulously carved lotus flower seat, standing a foot high, with an idol of Amman depicted in a beautiful, devotional manner. The goddess figure was elaborately decorated, wearing a crown, with splendidly crafted designs of jewels on the neck, arms, and legs. Her right leg rested on the stone stage, while the left was elegantly sculpted to be folded upon the lotus seat. The goddess's left hand was positioned on her legs on the lotus seat, holding a flower bud. Her right arm was raised, grasping a trident that was an inch thick and five feet tall, anchored into the stone stage.

Besides that, positioned ahead of the floral pedestal, a slender trident approximately a foot tall was embedded in the stone stage in front of the deity. The divine face of the goddess was adorned with sacred symbols, and her enchanting eyes compelled observers to bow and prostrate before her. Both friends were nearly in that state. They neglected their beedi packet, quickly concealed the disturbed bush area, placed the uprooted plants over it, and departed the location to resume their tasks.

All day long, the effect of the afternoon's occurrence weighed heavily on their thoughts. Even after completing their tasks in the evening, its influence lingered. They often pictured Amman in their imagination and were afflicted by an inexplicable emotion. The idol of the Goddess appeared to them in their dreams, leaving them restless even in sleep.

The following morning, they awoke knowing exactly what needed to be done. Together, they proceeded to the peepal tree at dawn. Armed with tools to cut through the thickets, they commenced their task before the sun rose. In two hours, they had fully cleared the bushes around the statue.

Once they finished their task, both were captivated by the sight of the Amman statue and the stone platform where it was set. They fully recognized the Goddess idol's divine beauty. At that moment, Mayan discreetly placed something into Soman's hands. Noticing it was the beedi pack they had lost on the first day, Soman tossed it away into a nearby bush. He then prostrated himself before the stone stage, bowing to the Goddess as it felt right to him. Mayan, always imitating Soman's actions, joined him and bowed to the Goddess.

After completing the morning's tasks, they returned to the Amman platform during the smoking break, holding only a matchbox without a beedi pack. With a clay lamp and oil in their hands, they approached the goddess, lit the lamp at her feet, and engaged in worship before returning with a sense of devotion.

The overnight devotion to Amman was new to them, but each time they encountered the goddess's statue, it reminded them of the Mariamman temple hall where they had resided years ago and the deity in that temple. They felt as if they had returned to the goddess. From that day onward, Soman developed the routine of lighting a lamp to the Goddess daily. Occasionally, Mayan would accompany him. However, Soman's lamp worship did not last long.

The rainy season was only a month away. Typically, normal life is disrupted by persistent rain during this season, lasting four to five months. Alan Williams was aware of this. He planned to select a hunting location in advance, once the boat was ready. Consequently, he headed to the lake's shore and began exploring the forested area. Soman had no choice but to accompany him. As they pushed the boat to the far shore, Mayan also joined in.

Their first try was unsuccessful, and no wildlife appeared before them despite their attempts. With just a week until the rainy season, Alan Williams one day learned about Soman's daily devotional practice and came directly to the lake shore to ask about it.

Finding only Mayan present, he inquired about Soman. Mayan indicated the peepal tree located at the peak of the mountain slope. Glancing that way, Alan Williams noticed Soman's activity there and proceeded to take Mayan with him to that spot.

Upon arriving at the peepal tree, he was astonished by the sight before him. Soman had illuminated a lamp in front of the goddess and embellished it with wildflowers. Alan Williams was awestruck by the stunning beauty of the Amman idol. Driven by curiosity, Alan attempted to ascend the stone stages to get nearer to the idol, but Soman promptly halted him, gesturing that he shouldn't step onto the platform with his shoes.

However, Alan Williams did not appear to be concerned. He ascended the stone platform without taking off his shoes, approached the idol closely, and examined it intently. Alan was amazed at the sculpture's beauty. Without hesitation, he circled the goddess, inspecting each detail of the idol, tapping some areas with his hands, and thought to himself that the entire piece was crafted from wood. Soman disapproved of Alan Williams's disrespectful behaviour, yet he remained inactive, unsure of how to prevent it. Just behind him, Mayan was equally taken aback. Both were certain of one thing: Alan Williams harboured some unsettling thoughts. They also realized they were powerless to stop it.

They were correct! Within two days, Alan Williams's actions validated their beliefs. From the moment he laid eyes on the statue, he had significant ideas brewing and chose to act on them. Neglecting his hunting trips, he commenced the project the day after seeing the statue, determined to finish it before the rainy season began.

Early that day, Alan Williams arrived at the peepal tree accompanied by five men. They brought the essential tools to take down the idol. Soman and Mayan trailed quietly behind, aware of the impending events. Alan Williams was unfazed by their presence and was determined to execute his scheme.

He provided instructions to the workers on how to remove the idol and instructed them to act accordingly. Alan Williams resolved that the statue must not incur even the slightest damage. Acknowledging that the situation was beyond control, Soman and Mayan went to sit beneath the peepal tree. They were indifferent but had no option but to watch passively.

The team began their task. Extracting the wooden statue from its stone pedestal proved more challenging than Alan Williams anticipated. The outcome was less successful than he desired, as a minor flaw remained at the end.

There was no trouble in detaching the idol from the stone platform with the lotus blossom seat. However, the removal of the Trident held in the right hand of the statue posed a challenge. The sculptors had arranged it in a highly intricate manner. Unaware of this, the statue was shifted and raised slightly above the stone platform in a hurry to declare the task complete. This led to the idol's damage.

The hand grasping the Trident detached from the idol and remained solely with the person holding the Trident. Observing this event, Alan Williams anxiously approached the individual with the Trident. The two friends seated under the peepal tree noticed that something unusual had occurred before them. They rose and proceeded to the stone stage immediately. By that time, Alan Williams examined how the Trident came to be on its own. He checked the location where it detached from the statue and the section connected to the Trident. He stood motionless for several minutes, overwhelmed with wonder. There was a reason for his intense astonishment.

The idol's right arm appeared severed as though the hand had been detached from the wrist without any small fragmentations. The separated hand remained gripping the Trident firmly. Alan Williams began investigating how this could have occurred. Once he grasped the complexities of the situation, his perplexity diminished, and he grinned, relieved that the issue could be resolved.

The artisans carved the palm section independently and connected it to the Trident, then fixed the Trident with the palm to the idol's right hand using a thin iron wire. The slender wire snapped, causing the wick to detach on its own. Everyone realized it immediately. The anxiety in Alan Williams's mind disappeared completely.

Deciding that the incident would not affect the implementation of the plan he had in mind, he ordered the servants to take the statue and the palm-jointed Trident to his house safely.

At that moment, Alan Williams observed a small, dusty, dirty stone with a dull red hue on the stone stage from which the statue had been removed. He bent down, picked it up, and held it in his palm, then briefly examined the statue's face. He realized that the stone might have been part of the idol's crown and had fallen off when the idol was moved. He instructed the four individuals carrying the idol to leave and gazed at the stone in his hand.

A standard round stone approximately half an inch wide. One face was rounded, while the other was flat. Upon lifting the stone toward the sunlight and peering at the sun through it, he pressed his lips together and deduced mentally that it could not be valuable. However, the carpenter nearby, holding the Trident detached from the Goddess idol, noticed the red stone in Alan Williams's hand illuminated by the sunlight, and his eyes gleamed.

Perhaps he was aware of the stone's worth! He quickly concealed his true feelings and appeared entertained by the events. Observing everything from the stone platform were Soman and Mayan. Alan departed, slipping the stone into his pocket and instructing the carpenter to deliver the Trident to the mansion.

Soman began to follow Alan Williams, with Mayan trailing behind as usual. After a brief distance, Soman ceased following them and returned to the stone stage holding Mayan's hand.

The two friends stood before the stone stage, which appeared empty in the absence of Amman. Alan Williams had left the slim, one-foot Trident standing in the middle of the stage. Soman picked up the clay lamp placed on the stone stage, set it in front of the small Trident, and lit it.

Did the tragic event he witnessed just moments before offer Soman a lesson, or did it evoke hope that the goddess's statue might return to that stone stage? For him, it was merely a light, but it brought peace to his mind. He then took Mayan and went back to work.

For a moment, there was quietness. The only noises were the rustling of the fig tree leaves and the birds chirping in it. The cool air might have been beneficial for them both. Malaimayan, with eyes shut, had halted narrating the story as he meandered through past events.

Absorbed in his tale, Raghavan, seated across from Malaimayan, rose and went into the house, intending to fetch water for him. Upon returning with the water, he found Malaimayan already inside. Malaimayan took the water from Raghavan, went to the home's front room, sat on the floor, and drank the water.

Will the old man leave without finishing the story? Raghavan found it reassuring that he was at home. Raghavan seated himself across from him. Malaimayan continued his tale.

The rainy season began with daily rainfall. Soman and Mayan became engulfed in their tea plantation tasks without any means of entertainment. They witnessed firsthand that the statue of Amman, enticed from beneath the peepal tree, had been transformed into a decorative piece in the mansion by Alan Williams.

Throughout the five-month rainy season, Soman and Alan Williams did not interact frequently. Alan Williams was fully absorbed in the task of finishing his mansion's construction. Nonetheless, he knew about Soman and Mayan's displeasure regarding the idol. After various attempts to pacify them, he conceived a new idea.

He truly wished the plan would alter their opinions. Consequently, his initial step was to wed Mayan to a woman employed at the tea estate. He housed the newlyweds in the mansion to assist him. As for Soman, he constructed a modest dwelling on the hillside slightly north of his mansion, married him to a girl working in a tea factory, and established them both there.

At that moment, Malaimayan paused the narrative once more, tapped the ground, and remarked, "This is the house. When he first settled into this place, he planted and nurtured the fig tree that has now grown in the backyard," and then he resumed the story.

Alan Williams's mansion was fully built. He resided alone in the vast mansion, except for Mayan and his spouse who lived in the small house constructed outside the mansion by Alan.

His duties included assisting Alan Williams and maintaining the mansion. Soman was employed at the tea estate and mill. Despite being apart, they reunited for hunting twice a week. Mayan's tasks involved more than just mansion duties; he also piloted the hunting boat, transported the animals they killed, and processed the animals into showpiece models that could be used as decorations.

With the tea estates and factories being efficiently managed by a competent team, Alan Williams found his sole leisure activity in hunting. His companions, who accompanied him, also became adept at assisting in the hunt. They spent half of the year hunting, and the other months were washed away by the rainy season. In the beginning, they hunted smaller animals, but as they gained expertise, they began to pursue larger and more dangerous prey.

Mayan was responsible for transporting all the hunted animals via boat to the mansion, where they were instructed on how to transform the deceased animals into lifelike replicas and assemble them in the mansion.

Over many years of hunting, the crafted animal decorations started to fill the designated hall in the house one by one. The heads of various animals were mounted on the walls of the reception area at the mansion's entrance. Entire animal figurines were stored in the internal animal hall.

Soman focused primarily on gardening and occasionally assisted Williams. As the years passed, he became preoccupied with his family duties. His son attended school in the nearby town up the hill. Both Soman and Mayan were in their late forties, while Alan Williams had surpassed fifty-five. Despite his age, his enthusiasm for hunting remained strong. However, their hunting days soon came to a screeching halt. Nobody anticipated it would end so cruelly.

And again, Malaimayan, who stopped the story, was sitting in the room gazing at the calendar he had viewed earlier that day.

Raghavan also glanced at the daily calendar and at Malaimayan's face. Malaimayan's heart burdened, and eyes distressed from the aftermath of a traumatic incident from years past. He gestured towards the calendar page and rose, stating that the event occurred on a new moon day much like today. Not prepared to divulge further, he declared, "I will return another day," and without waiting for Raghavan's response, he exited the house, moved towards the garden, and vanished.

Raghavan felt a deep disappointment. It seemed possible to him that his grandfather Somanathan was savagely murdered right before Malaimayan's eyes. But how did it happen? Who was responsible? Only Malaimayan could provide the answers once he spoke up again. The yearning to uncover the truth ignited in his heart. The secret remained hidden for the time being. Raghavan didn't see Malaimayan for several months, during which he had to concentrate on different matters, and, interestingly, he formed a new relationship.

Chapter 11

New Relationship

For over a month, Raghavan was unable to see Malaimayan. He intensely longed to hear the remainder of the tale and to learn the circumstances surrounding his grandfather Somanathan's death. Day after day, he waited for Malaimayan, only to feel let down. After several days, his interest waned, and he began focusing on other matters. He frequently visited Manikandan's shop. In the evenings, he would eagerly wait for Poonkuzhali to return from school to hear about the school events. The thought of the leopard, Uthamaraj was searching for occasionally came to his mind. However, according to Manikandan, Uthamaraj never returned to the shop. The days passed by without intrigue until that day added an exhilarating twist to life.

As Raghavan awoke in the morning, the dawn was already well upon the day. Sunlight poured over the mountainous region, visible through the window, marking the start of the day. The clear sky awaited the conclusion of the rainy season. A gentle breeze blew softly. Birds in the fig tree delightedly alternated between flying and perching on the branches, chirping joyfully. While reclining and observing all this, something unusual occurred in the fig tree at a height not visible through the window.

The bird's call jolted him awake, causing him to sit up from his reclined position. As he gazed through the window, something dropped from the uppermost branch of the tree and vanished from sight. Shortly afterwards, he noticed a wild cat descending the tree in a fierce manner, leaping from one branch to another.

Raghavan grasped the situation unfolding before him. The wild cat had struck a bird perched on a branch, and he witnessed the wounded creature plummet. With anxiety, he grabbed his crutch and hurried over to the window to examine the fig tree. Looking towards the tree's base, apprehensive that the cat might have seized the fallen bird, the sight was baffling to him.

The cat descended angrily and walked around the tree, searching for the bird that had fallen. He couldn't spot the bird and was unaware of what had become of it. However, this brought him some relief. He dashed out of the bedroom and raced to the backyard, hoping that if he was fast enough, he could rescue the bird.

As he reached and opened the backyard door, the cat had already noticed the bird. Fortunately for the bird, it was distant enough from the cat to avoid capture. Sensing the threat, the bird quickly slipped through a gap between the roots and concealed itself inside. The cat attempted to snatch the bird by sticking its forepaw into the hole.

Instantly realizing there was no immediate danger, Raghavan began contemplating how to chase away the stray cat. Standing on the doorstep, he raised his crutch and brandished it toward the cat, shouting, "Hey...! Shoo...! Go...!" The cat, lying on the ground with its legs spread out, turned its head at the sound coming from behind, attentively looked at Raghavan with its earlobes perked up, showing no fear.

Expecting the cat to flee upon hearing his shouts, Raghavan was somewhat taken aback by its fearless demeanour, which also irritated him. He proceeded to attempt to frighten the cat by waving the crutch in the air. The cat leapt once to dodge a potential blow, moved toward the left side of the fig tree, then paused, turned its head again, perked up its earlobes, slightly opened its mouth to display its sharp teeth, and growled to startle Raghavan.

Raghavan was further infuriated by the cat's behaviour, and in his anger, he resolved to somehow drive the cat away. He lifted his crutch high, preparing to descend the steps and confront the cat. However, in his haste, he stumbled, falling headfirst from the top of the steps and landing on the leafy ground beneath the fig tree. As he went down, the crutch he held slipped from his grasp, ending up near the wild cat, which was observing him from a short distance.

Startled by this sudden and unusual encounter, the cat quickly decided to flee, darting away on all fours. As Raghavan fell, he managed to lift his head slightly and saw the cat rapidly vanishing into the shrubbery.

With his fear of the cat gone, he turned his attention to the tree trunk, kneeling to investigate the fallen bird. He bent through the root opening, peering into the shadowy area like a cat on the prowl. Despite the morning light, it was quite dim inside. He could make out a bird hiding in a shadowy corner. Bringing his ear closer to the gap, he listened intently and detected a soft, painful "geek...geek..." sound. This faint noise led him to suspect that the bird within might be a parrot.

Carefully, he extracted the root beam and inserted his left hand inside, suffering a cut and a bite. The bird bit him. Undeterred, he reached further and gently removed the bird's body. The bird emitted a continuous cry of pain as he pulled. As he gradually brought it into the light, he recognized it as a parrot.

The parrot was persistently calling to him, continuously shaking its head and attempting to escape, despite his hold. The wound on its right wing was bleeding, turning the green feather blood red. Realizing he needed to treat it immediately, he grasped the parrot, picked up the crutch that had fallen under the tree, entered the house, and shut the door. He also closed the front door to ensure the parrot wouldn't escape.

He laid out a piece of cloth and carefully set the parrot down. Despite its injuries, the parrot attempted to fly, but its right wing had failed. When it tried to hop on its legs, it was even more unsuccessful, unable to move as its legs buckled, causing it to collapse and tumble over. It was only at that moment that he noticed the fracture just above the toes on the parrot's right leg, which was bent at an angle, a clear sign of the fracture.

Raghavan was at a loss, unfamiliar with any medical treatment. The only option he saw was to rush the parrot to the veterinary hospital in town. Determined to get medical assistance there, he retrieved a rattan basket from his home, lined the bottom with the cloth, and gently picked up the parrot, which was still rolling on the ground, placing it inside the basket and secured it. Holding the basket, he went to the door, mounted his two-wheeler with the basket in front of him, and departed. He was aware that the veterinary hospital was not far from the library. In his hurry, he forgot to lock his house, stopped briefly at Manikandan's shop to ask him to watch over the house, and then quickly headed towards town.

Manikandan couldn't comprehend Raghavan's behaviour; why was he in such a hurry? Where was he headed? What was in the basket? He had no answers to these queries. When the shop was devoid of customers, he went out onto the road, gazing in the direction Raghavan had departed. Manikandan spotted Raghavan returning around one in the afternoon.

Raghavan went straight to his house, parked his two-wheeler, and entered with the basket. He invited Manikandan, who had been following him, to come inside. Raghavan knelt in the front room, set the basket down, covered the parrot with a cloth, removed it, placed it on the floor, and uncovered it. Manikandan encountered the riddle that hadn't been disclosed until then. Overcome with emotion, he too knelt beside Raghavan to observe the parrot.

He had never observed a green parrot up close before. It was incredible to see a parrot for the first time with treated wounds and bandaged legs. The parrot was resting on its left side on the cloth beneath it. The injuries on the right wing were treated and the wing appeared in a yellowish-green hue. A small bandage covered the fracture on the right leg, and it lay in a dazed state, unable to bend its leg. It made no sound, exhausted from the treatment.

Raghavan asked, "Mani! If you have any millets in the store for the parrot, bring some." Manikandan promptly went, brought a paper packet, and opened it. He brought a mixture of rye, sorghum, and corn. Raghavan poured them into a bowl and placed it near the parrot's beak, adding water in another bowl.

The parrot did not eat anything. Leaving it as it was, he took Manikandan to the door and explained how the parrot had entered his house.

Raghavan entered the house after completing his tasks and once more sat beside the parrot. Despite the passage of time, the parrot was lounging in the same spot. As he sat down, he noticed it gazing at him with curiosity. He recalled some of the advice the veterinarian had given him during his visit to the clinic.

The wounds on the bitten wing would heal within two weeks. While the parrot would attempt to spread its wings and fly, the leg bandage would prevent flying. Wrap the wings in soft fabric to avoid them spreading. The bone in the leg would need at least a month to mend. During this period, keep the parrot safely in a cardboard box. Ensure that doors and windows remain shut to keep the cat from entering. The vet also recommended which foods to offer and which to avoid and advised returning for a follow-up in two weeks.

The unexpected bond with the wild parrot made Raghavan uneasy. In a few days, Raghavan devoted himself to its care, turning it into a full-time commitment, forming a friendship.

Chapter 12

Saru's Departure

Raghavan picked up a cardboard box from Manikandan's shop on the doctor's recommendation and placed the parrot inside. Feeling weary, he headed to the bedroom, lay down, and quickly drifted off to sleep. He was awakened by the sound of someone knocking at the door. Poonkuzhali stood at the entrance with a book bag slung over her back. Manikandan was with her, having just closed the shop. It was late in the evening. Poonkuzhali entered the house, nudged past Raghavan, made her way to the parrot's box in the living room, and looked inside. She jumped up twice with excitement, removed the bag from her shoulder, set it down, and knelt in front of the box, beginning to converse with the parrot as if she had been accustomed to doing so for quite some time.

She observed a nearby parrot for the first time. The parrot cocked its head, blinked, and attentively listened to the child speaking. Occasionally, it uttered a sound like 'kee... kee...' which surprised Raghavan. It seemed the parrot had gathered enough energy to vocalize. He moved the cereal bowl from the box closer to the parrot's beak. The parrot interacted with Poonkuzhali without physical contact.

Poonkuzhali took some millet from the bowl, held it in her palm, and used her left hand to bring the grains near the parrot's beak. The parrot began to nibble on the grains. Raghavan marvelled at the natural inclination women exude towards nourishing living beings. After feeding the parrot, Poonkuzhali returned home with a cheerful expression.

Following her example, Raghavan began to feed the parrot in the same way. For the next two weeks, he observed the parrot diligently. His main duties included cleaning and dressing the wounds three times daily, washing the food bowl, and providing fresh food.

In the evening, Poonkuzhali got off the bus and headed directly to Raghavan's house. She spent the entire evening with the parrot. Within two weeks, the injuries on the wing were fully healed. The doctor verified this at the clinic and advised being very cautious for an additional two weeks. He also cautioned him to ensure the parrot does not try to fly.

The following two weeks proved to be quite challenging for Raghavan. Despite having its wings restrained with soft fabric, the parrot attempted to fly and often collided with the box. Keeping the parrot inside the box became unmanageable since the fracture had somewhat mended, allowing it more mobility. It frequently scaled the box, leapt out, and tumbled. Raghavan spent all his time repeatedly returning it to the box. As he spent time with the bird, he unintentionally began conversing with it. A few days in, he realized the parrot needed a name; thus, the name Saru spontaneously came to him, and it stuck. By the end of the two weeks, Saru had ventured to various parts of the house, creating quite a bit of trouble for Raghavan.

During the final examination at the clinic, the doctor took off the bandages from the parrot's leg. After conducting some tests, he confirmed that the fracture had fully healed. He assured that from now on, it could fly without any hindrance. The doctor advised him to keep wild animals and birds in their natural habitats. He firmly instructed Raghavan to set the parrot free, allowing it to return to the place it was originally taken from.

Raghavan hesitated to follow the doctor's instructions. Over the past month, his minor connection with Saru had left him puzzled. He had begun to believe that Saru should remain with him. Even after returning from the hospital, he contemplated for a long time and didn't remove the cloth constraining its wings. Saru, having its leg bandages removed, began walking and hopping around the house with ease. But as it neared him, it collapsed and gazed at him in distress, unable to unfurl its wings, as if imploring, 'please set me free.' Raghavan, who had been enduring this and finding it amusing, realized in the evening and chose to set Saru free as the doctor had suggested.

Cradling Saru in his lap, he started to unwrap the cloth from around the wing. At that moment, a wave of sorrow enveloped his thoughts. The idea of Saru leaving him soon was unbearable. As the cloth fell away, he gently unfolded Saru's wings and set it on the ground.

It stood facing Raghavan, nodding its head up and down. Upon seeing this, Raghavan said "You can go". Saru seemed to understand and hopped a few steps. It then realized its wings were free, spread them, fluttered up, and perched on the curtain rod by the bedroom door. It turned its head to the side, keeping one eye on Raghavan before taking off, flying around the house briefly, and then returning to the curtain rod.

It was not until then that he realized both doors were shut. Raghavan quickly stood up, opened the courtyard's outer door, and motioned to the parrot, indicating a way out. If Saru grasped the gesture, it worked, as the parrot promptly flew off the rod and exited through the backyard gate the next moment.

Feeling as though he had misplaced something valuable, Raghavan quickly made his way to the backyard in search of Saru. To offer some solace, Saru was perched on a branch of the fig tree, announcing its presence with the sound 'kee… kee….' Raghavan approached, extending his left hand and calling out to Saru. Saru descended from the branch to settle on his hand, and Raghavan was overwhelmed with joy in that instant.

He gazed at Saru and pleaded, "No, don't leave. Stay with me," but as he spoke, Saru slipped from his grasp and returned to the tree branch. Meanwhile, in the distance, a flock of parrots was flying through the valley, their calls echoing. Saru instantly noticed the sound, turned her head toward it, and spotted Raghavan standing beneath the tree. Raghavan felt a pang in his heart, fearing Saru might join the group. It caused him to flutter with a gentle sadness welling up inside him.

With uncertainty clouding Raghavan's thoughts, he implored Saru once more, "Stay with me, don't leave," his voice choked with sorrow. Just then, the flock of parrots flew past the fig tree in the distance. At that moment, Saru sprang into the air and with a joyful cry of 'kee... kee... kee... kee...,' soared like an arrow towards the group. Raghavan watched as Saru swiftly flew ahead and merged with the others, and in no time, the entire flock vanished from view. The realization that he might never see Saru again weighed heavily on his heart, bringing tears to his eyes. Overcome with grief, he sank to his knees, clasped his stick before him, and rested his face against it. Tears fell from his eyes, landing onto the fig leaves on the ground.

A month may seem insignificant in a human lifespan, yet to Raghavan, the brief connection he formed with Saru during that month felt like years had gone by. He couldn't stand being apart from Saru. He had no idea how long he had been crying. He cried until his tears dried up, then settled beneath the fig tree and leaned against it. As the cool evening breeze enveloped him, he drifted off to sleep. Although the nap was brief, it successfully carried Raghavan into a world of dreams.

The sky teemed with thousands of parrots, all journeying in the same direction and chirping in unison. Raghavan flew alongside them in the flock, uncertain about the destination the parrots were heading towards. Swiftly, the birds soared into the clouds and ascended above them. The clouds appeared like fluffy bundles beneath. Trees, reaching up towards the heavens, scattered blossoms of Parijatham and coral jasmine upon him. He couldn't tell if it was night...! or day...! Raghavan imagined that the journey to paradise must be like this. Just then, he sensed something tugging at him from below, breaking his serene ascent in an undefined realm.

In that instance, all the parrots flying alongside him shattered into fragments and vanished abruptly. The trees overhead were nowhere to be seen. The clouds beneath also vanished. Poonkuzhali woke him up from his slumber under the fig tree. Coming directly from school, she entered Raghavan's house in search of Saru and Raghavan. In the open backyard, upon finding Raghavan asleep, she sensed that something unexpected had occurred, prompting her to wake him up quickly.

Raghavan, who unexpectedly arrived from the sacred route, was momentarily bewildered. He opened his eyes and saw Poonkuzhali in front of him, who asked, "Uncle, where is Saru?" Realizing what was happening, Raghavan collected himself after a moment and considered how to respond. When Poonkuzhali repeated her question, he answered, "Saru went to her house with her parents."

The child couldn't comprehend his words and questioned, "Where?" In response, Raghavan gestured towards the spot where the flock of parrots had vanished from his view. Poonkuzhali was equally puzzled. However, she realized that Saru was no longer there. She opened her palm and presented it to Raghavan, revealing the millets she held for Saru.

Wondering how to handle Poonkuzhali if she began to cry, he distracted her, saying, "Mama will search for you at home. Come on... let's get going," while holding her hands. Poonkuzhali released his hand, took several steps forward in the direction Raghavan indicated, and tossed the millets she held toward the sky. She returned inside, grabbed her book bag, and went to her house, holding Manikandan's hand as he stood at the door.

Raghavan, trailing her from behind noticed Poonkuzhali's tear-filled eyes. He grasped the bond Saru had formed over the month. If he himself couldn't stop the tears over Saru's departure, what could the poor young child do? He offered comfort to him.

Chapter 13

Jungle Journey

As soon as Raghavan got out of bed in the morning, he was seized by memories of Saru. The fig tree outside the window seemed to beckon memories, while the cardboard box in the front room reminded him of the month, he spent with Saru. The bird that had left him also affected Poonkuzhali's thoughts. Indeed, Saru had joyfully returned to her natural habitat, joining her fellow species. Raghavan was surprised to see her leave so happily, yet he cried uncontrollably, not fully grasping this reality.

He recalled a day when an elderly man, aged one hundred, was deeply upset over his friend of forty years who had shared his life. This realization helped Raghavan come to terms with Saru's departure as being expected. Simultaneously, reflections on Malaimayan disrupted Saru's recollections, bringing something to mind. This was due to Malaimayan having slipped from his thoughts for the last month.

The person who enthusiastically recounted old memories like a tale paused midway and mentioned he would return another day. However, he never did. Raghavan did not think about meeting him that month. He resolved to visit Malaimayan once more and needed to ask Manikandan about his location.

Maintaining his train of thought, he completed his morning tasks and approached the door. He noticed Manikandan's shop across the way. Customers were observed in the store. A dark green Jeep was parked on the dam road in front of the shop.

It crossed his mind briefly that one of the officers heading to the dam might have come to the shop, possibly the forest officer, Uthamaraj. He hurried excitedly toward the shop to inquire about the leopard, should it be him. Upon arriving and seeing the shop, he realized his suspicion was accurate.

Uthamaraj sat on the wooden bench at the shop's entrance, sipping tea. Raghavan approached, greeted him, and took a seat next to him. Noticing Raghavan, he greeted him warmly with a smile and resumed his conversation with Manikandan, asking, "then what happened?"

Manikandan responded, saying "the parrot flew away..." then gestured toward Raghavan, stating "he is here... ask him." At that moment, Raghavan realized they were discussing Saru's story. Uthamaraj instructed, "Give him tea as well," and then addressed Raghavan, "Alright, you tell me." Raghavan provided a brief account of the incidents that occurred from the time Saru came to him up until the day before it left. He couldn't disguise the sorrow on his face at that time.

The person who gently recognized the sorrow on Raghavan's face and gazed at him briefly said, "Raghavan! You did the right thing." He went on, "It's incorrect to believe that we should keep wild birds and animals with us for our enjoyment. Wild creatures are meant to exist in their natural habitat among their own kind. Our intrusion in their lives is detrimental to them and can sometimes become perilous for us as well. You shouldn't be concerned about." That concluded his brief speech.

He went on, "Listen Raghavan, my role involves safeguarding wild animals. We often rescue creatures that wander into human settlements and return them to their natural environment. Such occurrences are becoming common nowadays. Today, I'm planning to patrol the dam area. If you agree, I can bring you along. It might be a welcome change for you. If fortune Favors you, you might witness some wild animals in their natural surroundings. What do you think?" Uthamaraj concluded his remarks and gazed at Raghavan's face.

Raghavan raised his crutch as a response, indicating his disability. Not concerned by this, Uthamaraj reassured him by saying, "We're looking after you. We have four rangers accompanying us for protection."

Unsure of what to say, Raghavan glanced at Manikandan and signalled his willingness to join him. He was keen on it as well. "Alright, I'm coming. Let's go," he said as he stood up. Uthamaraj then suggested, "In that case, you'd better wear your military uniform." Raghavan agreed, saying, "I'll be back in five minutes," and cheerfully headed home. Shortly afterwards, Manikandan waved at Uthamaraj and Raghavan from within the shop as the jeep took off. At that moment, Raghavan was unaware that their journey would be perilous.

The journey in the Jeep along the paved embankment was incredible. They arrived at the dam in approximately fifteen minutes, traversing the steep route that wound between the tea plantation slopes. They needed to cross the embankment to reach the forested region on the other side. Once they passed through the security check at the embankment's entrance, the Jeep continued the roadway constructed on the dam.

To the right, the stored river water expanded, resembling a huge lake. On the left, the sluices released water that cascaded down in tiny waterfalls. The ears were entirely filled with the sound of these artificial waterfalls, and their continuous 'so...' sound dominated the mind. As they crossed each sluice, the clamour gradually faded, and their Jeep came to a halt at the security checkpoint on the other side of the embankment.

The guards greeted Uthamaraj and permitted his vehicle to go through. Uthamaraj steered the vehicle into the wooded area. The path was evident through the tracks left by the Jeep vehicle. As they followed these tracks, the noise of the water in the dam gradually diminished, allowing the profound quiet of the forest to envelop them.

In a matter of minutes, they arrived at their temporary dwelling, which felt close by. It was a small structure resembling a house, topped with an asbestos roof, and had only basic amenities. Four forest guards were already present, with one stationed on a watch tower roughly fifty feet ahead of the house. Everyone readied themselves to venture deep into the forest.

Initially, they tested their communication skills by inspecting the walkie-talkies they possessed. Positioned at the front of the jeep was a reclined seat with a man seated, holding a firearm. The other two entered the rear of the jeep, standing with weapons in their grips. To Raghavan, this setup appeared secure. The vehicle then set off towards the forest's interior, once more following the parallel tracks of the jeep path.

In just a few minutes, they were inside the thick forest. The path was bordered by dense trees and vines. Raghavan had the impression that it was still dark despite being morning. The vehicle jolted repeatedly as it navigated ditches, ridges, and stones. They were enveloped by a profound silence.

The occupants of the jeep remained silent thoroughly examining the area. They noted the absence of any animal activity. The bird calls were barely audible from afar. Raghavan also observing intently. His eyes revealed nothing. Subsequently, the vehicle's pace was slowly decreased, and it came to a halt along the path.

Uthamaraj halted the vehicle and gestured towards a branch on the side. Raghavan noticed a hornbill perched there, nibbling on fruit with its elongated beak. It was Raghavan's first time seeing the bird, and it appeared both beautiful and unusual. The bird's beak stretched half the length of its body. Observing the people below, it silently unfurled its large wings and took flight.

Once more, the travel persisted in silence, wordlessly. Raghavan was bored, feeling like he was traversing an endless forest. The moment the forest ranger at the front of the vehicle lifted his right hand and signalled, Uthamaraj reduced the vehicle's speed and came to a halt.

The lead man gestured towards the path ahead, indicating where to focus their attention, and everyone turned their gaze to that spot. Raghavan was unaware of anything there. Nevertheless, they observed the area intently. Despite that, Raghavan still couldn't perceive anything there. However, everyone except Raghavan, who was patiently waiting, seemed to know what was about to occur.

Raghavan stood by with anticipation, just as they did. In no time, their prediction came true. About a hundred meters away on the path of Jeep, the vegetation on the right side rustled, and an elephant gradually emerged. A colossal shape, roughly ten feet in height, appeared from the undergrowth and blocked the path.

The elephant nodded its head and lifted its trunk, waving it in the air inexplicably, then slowly crossed the path just as it had approached, vanishing among the trees on the other side. Was what Raghavan witnessed real? He couldn't believe it. He was amazed that such an enormous creature appeared briefly and disappeared. To him, it seemed as if a dim black barrier, as though the entire body was dusted in ash, briefly obstructed the path.

He had observed large elephants in temples before. Nonetheless, witnessing the wild elephant right in front of him and its gestures thrilled him. His wonder continued. Once more, the vines shifted to the right, and a second elephant emerged, following the first one and crossed the path.

After that, elephants emerged individually and in small clusters from the right side of the trail, traversing the elephant path diagonally to intersect with the human path. The spectacle of numerous elephants passing by with their young captivated their eyes. Raghavan watched, forgetting to blink. Meanwhile, others waited somewhat uninterested for the entire elephant herd to cross, as if the scene was quite mundane.

Realizing the moment they had waited for had come, they got ready to depart. The path appeared vacant as all the elephants had already passed. Still, they remained calm, keeping the vehicle steady. As anticipated, within a few seconds, another elephant emerged and stood on the path, just like the first. It looked to both sides of the path but did not cross along the herd's route ahead. A vehicle halted on the left, and some people inside seemed to unsettle it. Facing the jeep, it began to move.

With that, everyone in the jeep, apart from Raghavan, prepared for the next move in their individual way. Uthamaraj started the vehicle and got ready to shift into reverse gear. Despite this, the elephant continued approaching. The two security guards at the back quickly leapt from the jeep and joined the guard at the front. They appeared fearless.

Yet the previous situation was unfamiliar and distinct for Raghavan. He encountered numerous threats during his time in the army. His existence revolved around explosives and detonations. He never had the chance to be at the war front either. All his perils were related to material aspects.

A wild elephant was in front, approaching him. He couldn't even exit the vehicle to flee. Yet, the courage of the forest guards was remarkable. Even as they courageously faced the elephant, it gave him no comfort. Raghavan sat inside the vehicle, his hands, and thighs trembling. His heart pounded with anticipation of the unforeseen event. However, what happened in the following moments left him utterly astonished.

Chapter 14

Wild Elephant

The elephant was moving forward. The individual seated at the front of the vehicle also leapt out, and the three forest rangers positioned themselves a few paces in front of the elephant. Inside the jeep, Raghavan felt anxious about the next sequence of events. The trio of guards in front lifted both arms with guns and began yelling in an unintelligible language. Simultaneously, Uthamaraj began to reverse the vehicle. The elephant approaching the jeep suddenly paused. Its head then jerked violently from side to side, repeatedly raising its trunk. The elephant then retreated from the path, rejoining the other elephants that had crossed earlier, and disappeared as if nothing had occurred.

Once the elephant vanished from view, they lingered in the same spot for a few minutes, observing the path it had taken in hopes it might return. Eventually, they showed a sense of relief. They resolved to move on and continued their trek. Raghavan was concerned about the considerable distance he had travelled into the forest and the need to retrace his steps to return.

If his unexpected escape from the elephant was astonishing, the actions of the elephant were even more incredible. The other four individuals in the jeep conversed casually and quietly, as if nothing had transpired. He was curious about their actions and asked, "Why didn't you fire the gun? How did you manage to drive the elephant away by shouting in some language?" They chuckled and explained, "The sound of gunfire can provoke any animal to act aggressively. It involves significant risk. In such situations, it's strategic to make it seem like we do not fear the animals. That's precisely what we did," explained the forest guards.

They went on to say, "We've observed the hill residents by the dam do the same. We picked it up from them." They also mentioned, "There's no need to worry, we're heading back to the dam now. We should get there in thirty minutes," which brought relief to Raghavan.

They remained silent until they returned to the watchtower area. Uthamaraj, accompanied by Raghavan, drove towards the embankment, leaving three guards stationed at the house. Uthamaraj began to regret bringing Raghavan, feeling it was a mistake. His fear had subsided, and he felt a responsibility to ensure Raghavan's safe return home. However, the threat was not yet over.

After they crossed the embankment once more, Raghavan returned to his usual self, as the events in the forest faded from memory. He felt relieved as he reached the hill town road. However, his fear resurfaced when he noticed a sign nearby. The 'Jeep' ascended with a warning sign in view: 'Caution! Elephants Cross…!' Considering asking Uthamaraj about it, he turned to face him. But failing to comprehend the confusion on Uthamaraj's face, he focused on the road ahead. Suddenly, his body tensed as he grasped the situation. At that moment, Uthamaraj decelerated and promptly parked the jeep by the roadside. Just fifty feet ahead, they witnessed the sight again of elephants moving from left to right across the tarmac.

In that perilous setting, it was intriguing to watch the young cubs eagerly darting amongst the large elephants, who moved with composure. Uthamaraj settled his hands on the steering wheel before him and remarked to Raghavan, "There's no need to fear the elephant herd; it's the solitary ones that are dangerous." Just then, a noise from behind startled them both.

Raghavan promptly glanced back at the jeep together with Uthamaraj. The sight unsettled him. A male elephant, with two sharply curved upward tusks, was accelerating, thrashing its trunk in various directions and vigorously shaking its head. Realizing the urgency to act quickly before the elephant caught up to them, Uthamaraj abruptly leapt out of the jeep. Immediately after jumping, he lifted both his hands and executed the same tactic the forest guards had used in the forest earlier that day.

The elephant approaching from the right side of the paved road noticed the vehicle stationed on the left. As the male elephant was rushing to reunite with the herd, a man appeared in its path with arms extended, seemingly causing a bit of alarm, prompting the elephant to alter its route towards him.

Uthamaraj's brave gesture of raising his arms did not deter the elephant, which advanced toward the jeep, frightening him. When the elephant was just twenty feet away, Uthamaraj quickly ran to the front of the jeep and concealed himself from the elephant's sight behind a roadside tree.

Raghavan sat inside the jeep, pale-faced and trembling, with no fear left of elephants or for his own life. In his utmost despair, he was frozen, observing the elephant as it neared the jeep. Once the man who drew attention with his arm-waving vanished into the trees, the elephant paused for a moment by the jeep, eventually turning its focus to Raghavan inside.

Raghavan was paralyzed with fear, unable to make a sound. The elephant shoved the jeep from the driver's side, causing it to tip over. Uthamaraj, observing from behind a tree, bravely decided to rescue Raghavan from the elephant. He stepped out from his hiding place and yelled at the elephant with cries like hey...! Ah....! Uh....! and clapped loudly to draw its attention away.

His efforts paid off. Upon seeing the man again, the elephant ceased pushing the jeep and began approaching him. Uthamaraj began to run upon spotting the elephant, intending for it to follow him. As he planned, the elephant started pursuing him. Meanwhile, Raghavan exited the jeep and headed towards its rear.

He intended to conceal himself behind the trees nearby, but as he quickly moved, the crutch struck the jeep, producing a 'Thud' sound. The sound drew the elephant's focus back to the jeep, causing it to disregard Uthamaraj, who had begun running ahead. Raghavan, positioned behind the jeep with a stick in his hand, became the focus. The elephant gradually rotated and moved toward Raghavan, shaking its head.

Raghavan stumbled backwards using a crutch, standing by the roadside as he watched the elephant draw near. The elephant passed the jeep and veered in Raghavan's direction. Only a few paces away stood the edge of the road, and a large crater loomed behind him. Raghavan realized that the end of his time was imminent.

As a last measure, he resorted to using Uthamaraj's tactic and began speaking to the elephant in a booming voice while grasping the crutch in the middle and exclaimed, "Hey…! You…! You're not alone! Your herd is over there...", motioning to the right, "Head over there...!" he continued. Then, pointing to Uthamaraj on the left, who was observing the scene, he added, "Go to him…! He's a Forest officer. Don't come to me. I'm a soldier… I'm alone…!" He began to mumble incoherently.

The elephant observed Raghavan's movements and shook its head, then advanced two paces towards him, lifted its trunk, and let out a powerful roar. Abruptly, the impact from the elephant hitting him made Raghavan stagger. He retreated a step and continued. Next thing, he toppled backward into the ditch. The crutch remained at the roadside.

When the man ahead suddenly vanished, the elephant backed away, appearing a bit perplexed, and paused in the roadway. What went through its mind? Perhaps its herd was crossing. It hurriedly moved on, paying no attention to the forest officer observing the scene anxiously at the roadside.

Free from his fear of the elephant, Uthamaraj hurried to the location where Raghavan had fallen. At the brink of the ditch where Raghavan had tumbled, he looked down and saw nothing but vines.

Recognizing the urgent situation, Uthamaraj dashed to activate the walkie-talkie in the vehicle and quickly chose to save Raghavan. After notifying the rescue team and his assistants, the forest guards, Uthamaraj returned to the pit where he had fallen and shouted his name loudly, listening for any reply. There was no reply. Exhausted as he was, he took the crutch from the ground and approached the 'Jeep,' leaning on it as he nervously awaited help. The fading evening light only heightened his anxiety.

Assistance he was anticipating finally came. Upon arriving at the scene, the forest guards commenced their search effort without delay. Lacking the proper equipment, they were unable to descend into the expansive crater. Eventually, the rescue squad appeared, further escalating the efforts to save Raghavan.

The rescue team swiftly climbed down into the trench and discovered Raghavan suspended from a tree branch twenty feet below, then safely brought him to the surface. The accompanying doctor promptly checked the unconscious individual, stating, "He lost consciousness due to a head injury. He only sustained minor bruises on his knees." Uthamaraj was visibly relieved upon hearing this.

They quickly placed him in the jeep and took him home. The doctor settled him in his bedroom, checked his wounds again, cleaned, and dressed the one on his head. After treating the bruises on his leg, he remarked, "That will do." At this point, Raghavan, although still unconscious, began to move his arms and legs.

The doctor accompanying them assured, "There's no need to worry. Remove the bandages from the head tomorrow morning and apply this medication." He handed over the medicine as well. He instructed, "Use the same on the leg," before departing with the rescue team. Uthamaraj positioned himself by Raghavan's feet on the bed and waited for him to regain consciousness. Meanwhile, Manikandan's family arrived upon hearing the news. Poonkuzhali sat near Raghavan's head, watching him with concern.

Upon awakening from his fainting spell, Raghavan's eyes first registered Poonkuzhali's sorrowful expression. He pondered, 'Why is Poonkuzhali present here?' As these thoughts crossed his mind, he noticed Uthamaraj seated in front of him, which triggered a gradual recollection of past events. He recalled the encounter with the elephant, then remembered being airborne before abruptly colliding with something and injuring his head. However, he had no recollection of how he made it back home after that.

He couldn't remember falling backward into the ditch when he heard the elephant's piercing call, injuring his right knee on a jagged tree branch, banging his head on the tree trunk, passing out, and dangling upside down like a bat until the rescue team arrived to retrieve him. Uthamaraj gazed at Raghavan and reassured, "Don't worry, I'll return tomorrow to explain everything that happened," and instructed Manikandan to look after Raghavan.

The following morning, Raghavan removed the bandages from his head wound and tended to it with medicine. After having the breakfast provided by Chitra, he waited for Uthamaraj. He had already been informed about everything that transpired on the first day. He resolved not to hold Uthamaraj responsible for the events that occurred. As a forest officer, encountering wildlife is expected. However, he felt it was an error to get involved in his work. It was completely clear how accurate his words about Saru were. He was pleased that Saru had returned to its natural habitat.

Uthamaraj arrived and asked about his well-being, expressing regret for the mishap on the first day. Raghavan kept it honest, expressing gratitude by acknowledging his attempts to help. After conversing with Raghavan for a bit, Uthamaraj headed to the door, with Raghavan following him. There, Raghavan's eyes widened in astonishment.

Malaimayan approached from the direction of Manikandan's residence. By the time Uthamaraj departed, Malaimayan had already passed the buildings and went directly to him. He entered, seated himself in the hall, and asked Raghavan to come inside. His visit wasn't for a health check-up. There was an urgent tension about him, and with that same tension, he spoke, "Brother Raghava, you are fortunate. I need to share a secret I've kept in my mind for quite some time." He paused.

"Grandpa, why are you speaking like this? Is something wrong?" When Raghavan posed this question, Malaimayan responded in a manner that Raghavan couldn't comprehend,

"You're the one fit for it. I must inform you. Be at the lakeside tomorrow morning," he instructed before leaving."

Even after his departure, the words he had spoken reverberated. Raghavan was pondering the meaning behind the statement that he was 'fortunate'. Was he referring to his narrow escape from being trampled by an elephant? Or was he referring to being chosen for the secret he was about to bestow upon him? Regardless, one thing was certain. Raghavan held onto the hope that the following day might uncover the mystery surrounding his grandfather Somanathan's demise.

Chapter 15

Somanathan's Sacrifice

Raghavan received his breakfast from Manikandan's house, aware that this arrangement would persist until his recovery. After finishing his meal, he prepared to meet Malaimayan. He remembered Malaimayan's invitation to "Come to the lakeshore," which meant he didn't have to search for him. However, to get to the lakeshore, he needed to descend to the valley's bottom. Despite the challenging trek, his curiosity about the secret Malaimayan promised to reveal compelled him.

Raghavan exited the house and began his walk toward Manikandan's residence. To reach the base of the valley, the route led beyond Manikandan's place and through the tea garden. While passing by the line of houses, he saw children playing with the ball he had purchased for them. Observing them, he realized that two of the children were of school-going age that year. Taking a mental note to enrol them in a school, he continued down to the tea garden. The path through the valley was narrow as it descended. He perceived the distance as a major challenge and slowly made his way downwards.

With the onset of the cold season, the sun shone in the sky, yet its warmth was absent. A mild chilly breeze swept through, causing a shiver. In such surroundings, Raghavan arrived at the foothills with little exhaustion and paused for a short while, losing himself in the scenic beauty of the valley lake.

Spanning at least half a kilometre, small waves formed on the lake's surface and were propelled by the wind. The lush green grass, extending from the lakeshore to where he stood, also danced in the wind's direction, creating a captivating sight. Raghavan navigated through the ankle-deep grass to arrive at the lake's edge.

The lake's waves crashed onto the shore, producing sounds like 'click...' and 'clack...' while splashing up foam. Raghavan leaned forward with enthusiasm to reach the water. As he bent closer to the lake, a noise behind caught his attention, prompting him to glance back while in his crouched position. With hands motioning as if signalling no, Malaimayan was approaching quickly, sprinting, and strolling across the grass.

Malaimayan approached Raghavan, took his hand, and led him about ten feet away from the edge of the lake, asking him to sit on the grass. Once Raghavan settled down, Malaimayan also sat down beside him. After a silent moment, Malaimayan gestured toward the bank where Raghavan had previously stood and spoke in a light voice, "Thirty years ago, we sacrificed your grandfather, Soman, at this spot. Now that you're here, I'm frightened," he explained for his actions.

"How?" was the sole question Raghavan posed. "I've come to tell you something," Malaimayan responded softly. He readied himself to share the rest of his tale, sitting upright with his legs crossed. He started narrating, closing his eyes to remember past events and opening them as he spoke. Raghavan began to piece together the disjointed sentences from Malaimayan, mentally connecting the events and filling in the gaps with his imagination.

The yearly rainy season had started. Continuous rain throughout the day disrupted numerous tasks in the tea garden. However, activities within the mansion continued. Mayan and his wife were constantly assisting Alan Williams. Soman was occupied with duties both in the garden and at the mill. Additionally, he took an active interest in his son Devanathan's school education.

Hunting ceased during the rainy season. During this period, Alan Williams focused on enhancing the mansion's appearance. Each arrangement and decoration were carried out under his supervision. The interior design and decorative elements not only gave the mansion a grand feel but also introduced an element of dread. The reception room was spacious, featuring curved staircases on either side that ascended to the upper levels. The area at the intersection of these staircases on the first floor resembled a hall.

Extending from that upper corridor, Alan Williams's chamber took up the rear portion of the mansion on a spacious floor. The windows in his room offered a view of the entire mountain area. Below his room was a large hall of equal size, where they stored all the processed skins and the models of the animals they had hunted.

Mayan was responsible for crafting puppets resembling live animals, which he showcased in the back of the animal hall. He had already arranged the heads of different animals in the reception area at the home's entrance. The walls of the room featured mounted deer heads with antlers and bison heads. In certain spots, he also included iguanas and snakes to enhance the ominous atmosphere of the front hall.

Alan Williams, with great care and responsibility, removed the Amman statue from its stone pedestal and beautifully enshrined it inside the mansion. Situated on the first floor, the statue of Amman is visible right from the mansion's entryway. Positioned on the edge of the floor above the rear section of the main reception hall, the goddess's statue faces the front door, reducing the mansion's ominous presence and fostering a feeling of safety.

The goddess statue's Trident and the hand holding it were expertly repaired and positioned, giving the impression that the goddess was seated with the Trident. The red gem that had dislodged from the crown was also reattached and polished.

Creating animal models and showcasing them in the exhibit area beneath Alan Williams's room was Mayan's primary occupation. He was constantly working with animal hides and sewing tools like needles and leather threads. Most of his hours were spent within the mansion. He possessed a box filled with glass eye shapes of diverse designs and hues for animal figurines, alongside a collection of nails and teeth from various creatures.

Mayan's wife assisted Alan Williams and him in crafting these model animals, except while she was cooking. They worked together to turn the animal hall into an impressive exhibition hall filled with animal models. The whole mansion was filled with the animals they created, and before long, it became known as the 'hunting mansion' in the region.

Mayan occasionally joined Soman for leisure activities. Usually around midday, they headed to the stone platform by the mansion and relaxed for a bit. They used to smoke cigars during these moments. What was once a beedi was now a cigar. The stone platform, originally a shrine for the deity, had transformed into a recreational spot.

The rains had ended, ushering in the winter season. Construction on the hunting lodge was halted. Despite his age, Alan Williams was getting ready for a hunting expedition. He paid no heed to Mayan's warning about the lack of space for additional animal trophies in the hunting room. Alan chose to embark on a hunting trip that weekend, ignoring Soman's advice that, for the sake of his health, he should perhaps cease hunting activities.

At the lake's edge, an issue confronted the trio following Williams's hunting plan. Recent rainfall had triggered a new flood in the river, causing the lake's water level to surge significantly. The dock along the lake's bank was underwater, with the boat afloat in the lake. Soman and Mayan entered the lake, retrieved the boat to shore, and then needed to proceed to the far shore.

The hunt that day ended prematurely. A black panther, limping for some reason, was caught. Alan Williams shot it without facing any opposition. They struggled to lift the dead panther onto the boat and made their way to the shore, where they needed to remove the dead panther from the boat.

All three were extremely fatigued. Alan Williams dismissed Soman's suggestion to fetch additional people. Nevertheless, the trio attempted to drag the boat from the water, aiming to complete the task according to Alan Williams's directives. They were unable to pull the boat entirely from the water, leaving it partially submerged and partially on the shore, after which the three men lifted the dead leopard.

Alan Williams was in knee-level water beside the boat, holding the leopard, when he suddenly cried out due to sharp pain in his ankle. His cries persisted as he couldn't endure the agony of pulling his leg. Soman, nearby with the leopard, was puzzled by Williams's cries, abandoned the leopard to assist him. However, when Alan Williams slipped from his grasp and fell into the water, Soman was horrified to realize what was happening to his legs. A crocodile had seized his leg and was dragging him into the water.

Alan Williams fainted from the pain. Meanwhile, Mayan arrived to assist from the other side of the boat. Soman asked him to support Williams, then leapt and retrieved Williams's gun from inside the boat. Despite his lack of shooting experience, he jammed the gun's muzzle between the crocodile's jaws and fiercely jabbed. This action caused the crocodile to release Alan Williams's leg and move back slightly.

Soman instructed Mayan to quickly drag Williams to the shore, while he himself assisted by lifting Williams from behind and pushing him to safety. The crocodile, which had momentarily retreated, swiftly turned and lunged at Soman. With a single powerful move, it seized Soman's right thigh and dragged him into the water. Too fatigued to resist, Soman sank into the water with the firearm. In no time, Soman disappeared, and the crocodile was also absent from the scene.

Mayan pulled Williams to the shore and left him gazing back at it in confusion. On the lake's edge, the boat rocked with the black leopard in it. Soman was gone. The splashes of blood-streaked lake water on the shore served as the only testimony to the tragedy that occurred there.

After some time, a commotion appeared in the water at a distance in the lake. There, Mayan noticed a crocodile contorting itself, with human body parts swirling alongside it. Within a few minutes, the disturbance also ceased, leaving the lake calm.

Seeing Alan Williams unconscious with blood oozing from his leg onto the grassy ground, along with the aftermath of the lake massacre, jolted Mayan out of shock. He began shouting and raced towards the hunting mansion to seek assistance.

Malaimayan's body shook. His eyes filled with tears that rolled down his cheeks. Raghavan also shivered as he thought about his grandfather's violent death. The sudden loss left him deeply affected. Raghavan waited a considerable time for the sobbing to cease. Malaimayan was unable to escape the influence of those sorrowful memories.

The sun was hidden by clouds, and darkness enveloped the area. Suddenly, Malaimayan stood up and began walking across the grass toward the slope of the tea garden. Raghavan got up too and went after him. Unable to match Malaimayan's pace, he walked slowly. By then, Malaimayan had vanished into the tea plantation slope. Even upon reaching the mountain's summit, Malaimayan was nowhere in sight. The events that followed would be known only when Malaimayan returned to recount them. Raghavan then made his way back to his home.

Chapter 16
Death of Alan Williams

At the onset of winter, the weather turned extremely cold and snowy. Raghavan found himself confined at home. Despite the months that passed, Raghavan had no opportunity to meet Malaimayan again since their last encounter by the lakeshore. Raghavan frequently visited Manikandan's shop. On that day, Raghavan made his way to the door. The road in front of the dam was obscured by fog, making it invisible. Regardless of the heavy snowfall, Manikandan kept his shop open. He never closed it, no matter how severe the rain or snow. Raghavan decided to visit Manikandan's shop, donned his winter apparel, and set out.

When he got there, the store was devoid of customers. Manikandan felt pleased to see Raghavan. He seated him and prepared tea for the two of them. Carrying two cups of tea, he descended from the shop and joined Raghavan. Raghavan inquired about his earlier thoughts. "You continue to keep the shop open even during harsh weather with heavy rain and snow. If there are no customers, then shut the shop."

As he sipped his tea, Manikandan told Raghavan, "I mentioned to you the other day that even if the shop stays open all day, there won't be much business. This shop is meant for public welfare and doesn't really have holidays. I will only close it for something important. Otherwise, it stays open during daylight." He added, "Even if I'm not here, people will manage the business on their own." Raghavan recalled how once, two women took care of things just as he had said, so he acknowledged, "Yes, I've observed that, Mani…"

Manikandan had more to share, "This small shop has a past, are you interested?" Without pausing he added, "You're free at the moment, pay attention." He began narrating the shop's history.

"Your grandfather Somanathan discovered my father lost and orphaned in the shopping street and brought him to Athimedu. At that time, he was fifteen years old. After working in the tea plantations for a few years, he engaged with the locals and initiated a shop catering to the community's needs. Initially, he bought the shop's required goods at public expense and entrusted them to my father. It was planned that my father would operate the shop entirely on his own within a year or two. Up until that point, your grandfather would cover the daily expenses. Sadly, your grandfather passed away unexpectedly just as your father completed his education." Raghavan recalled the event by the lake and felt a slight tremor through his body, which he quickly concealed.

Manikandan went on to say, "After that, your father had to discontinue his studies and took a job at the tea factory. The shop remained a general welfare outlet. I'm taking over after my father." Pausing, he added, "Raghava, there's no profit from this shop. The locals rely on it. I'm glad to meet their needs. This life suffices for me. I enjoy it," he finished.

Raghavan internally praised him and reflected, 'What sort of person..., he led a simple life serving others without looking for anything in return.'

Raghavan recalled Manikandan bringing up his grandfather's death. He considered that Manikandan might know everything, and it appeared to Raghavan that the unspoken words of Malaimayan could be understood through him. He then approached him about the matter. "Do you know how my grandfather Somanathan passed away?" Raghavan questioned quickly.

As Raghavan awaited a response from Manikandan, the reply came, "I am aware of your grandfather's passing, the death of that white man, and your father's as well. I have never disclosed to you how your father died, although I intended to convey this to you eventually." He proceeded, "However, before I share that, I must advise you to distance yourself from that elderly man. It is not beneficial for you. Four days ago, you were observed by the lake with him." Manikandan paused and emphasized, "Steer clear of him immediately."

Disregarding Manikandan's urgent advice, Raghavan bluntly asked, "Why?" Manikandan, slightly irritated, replied, "You'll only understand the situation if I explain it to you." He went on, "Listen, Raghava! This area is under a curse. The deity 'Soolamuni' frequently possesses Malaimayan. During such times, he gains the strength of an elephant, attacking and killing anyone nearby. Some say that 'Soolamuni' through Malaimayan caused your father's death." By the end of his explanation, fear was evident on his face.

After listening for a while, Raghavan asked with a neutral expression, "Soolamuni? Who is that?" Manikandan, irritated, replied, "Everyone around here knows this, don't you know anything?"

With the same fury, he described, a large peepal tree, a kilometre south of their house, underneath it, on a stone platform, was a slender Trident that was Soolamuni. He went on to explain that promptly at noon, Soolamuni arrives on horseback. As the horse gallops, its sound reverberates through the valley. What could be more astonishing! Soolamuni then secures the horse to the peepal tree, enjoys a cigar on the stone platform, and eventually rides off, vanishing from sight. Manikandan, clearly flustered, began to perspire as he relayed this story.

"Who provided you with this information? Did you witness it?" Raghavan queried. "You won't believe it, but I witnessed it firsthand," Manikandan immediately responded. "It occurred after your father passed away a year ago. It was noon when I brought lunch to Chitra and then returned," he paused. "Is that so?" Raghavan prompted him to go on. Looking at Raghavan, "I noticed cigar smoke emanating from behind the Trident. I quickly left the area out of fear." He began to counsel him, "Raghava! During midday, no one visits the stone stage. The old man with the hammer is said to be there at that hour. That's what people who have witnessed it say. Avoid that path," he concluded."

Raghavan was skeptical about Manikandan's words, suspecting them to be mythical. His curiosity to uncover the truths left unspoken by Malaimayan grew. However, the moment and setting to do so did not present themselves right away.

The following morning, Raghavan awoke and glanced out the window at the sky. It was cloudless and clear. The first hints of sunrise appeared in the eastern sky as daylight started to expand, and birds began their movement through the valley. Birds were also chirping in the fig tree.

He believed he needed to locate Malaimayan to extract the remainder of the story from him. An idea struck him. Since Malaimayan might visit Manikandan's house to obtain a cigar, he could trail him and catch up with him by the stone stage. To do so, he completed his morning tasks swiftly and settled onto the cement slab at the entrance shed, keeping an eye on Manikandan's house.

After some time, Poonkuzhali emerged, holding her book bag. She had on a winter coat that covered her head. Approaching Raghavan's house, she felt glad to see him and hurried to Manikandan's shop. Watching her, he thought she would complete her first grade in two months. Poonkuzhali and a few other children got on the bus at the dam. Raghavan stood up, exited the tent, and waved to the children on the bus. He returned to the shed, took a seat on the bench, and looked towards Manikandan's house.

Raghavan watched with anticipation as Malaimayan made his way through the distant tea plantation. He prepared himself. The moment Malaimayan received a cigar from Chitra and turned, Raghavan began to follow. He quickened his pace, determined to meet him at the stone stage no matter what.

Upon reaching the stone platform as quickly as possible, Malaimayan was nowhere to be seen. The cigar was placed in front of the Trident on the stone platform. Despite thoroughly searching the area, there were no indications of Malaimayan's presence. Raghavan was forced to leave feeling disappointed.

While he lay in bed, disheartened by the failure of his morning attempts, an idea suddenly struck him in the afternoon. It was nearly twelve by then. 'What if he heads to the stone stage now?' This thought quickly transformed into action, and he promptly got up and prepared to head to the stone stage. He recalled Manikandan's warning about avoiding that place at noon. However, a peculiar boldness overtook him, and he left without heeding the warning.

While he advanced toward the stone stage with some bravery, the dread of Soolamuni persistently lingered in the back of his mind. As he approached the stone stage, his steps gradually lost their firmness. He reached the peepal tree just in time. The tree's shadow cast a dimness over the area, making it appear slightly dark. The tree's branches and leaves were still. Not a breeze stirred. Silence enveloped everything, a profound silence. Raghavan, who had arrived hoping to meet Malaimayan, felt let down once more upon realizing he wasn't there.

He maintained a distance before the stone platform and gazed at the Trident situated directly ahead of him. No occurrences unfolded as Manikandan had described. It was at this moment he realized the absence of the cigar in front of the

Trident. He trembled slightly and retreated a couple of steps. Inspecting beneath the peepal tree, he found no horse. The wonder manifested itself only when he observed the Trident once more.

'Shirr...' He perceived the crackle of flames from the Trident and kept his gaze fixed on it. Soon after, smoke started rising from behind the Trident, accompanied by the scent of a cigar. He was baffled by the unfolding events. Like Manikandan, he was also witnessing the same spectacle described. While Manikandan managed to leave the scene immediately, Raghavan was unable to do so. Firmly pressing his crutch into the ground, Raghavan slightly lost his balance. The faint sound from his misstep caused yet another marvel in that moment, leaving him astonished.

Malaimayan quietly rose from the back of the stone stage, standing behind the Trident with a lit cigar in his hand. He stood up, glanced back, and exclaimed, "Oh you!" With that, he moved forward around the stone stage, seated himself on it, placed the cigar in his mouth, and inhaled deeply. The cigar's tip glowed red before dimming. Smoke drifted out from his mouth, creating an image in Raghavan's mind of a skeleton enjoying a cigar.

As soon as he understood that the cigar smoke originated from Malaimayan, his bewilderment vanished. However, he couldn't grasp the reason for the theatrics. With a clear mind, Raghavan strolled over and seated himself beside the stage, positioning himself a few feet away from Malaimayan to avoid the cigar smoke.

After a few moments of quiet, Raghavan asked, "Grandpa, why are you hiding and smoking a cigar like this?" Malaimayan looked at Raghavan for a while without responding directly, then turned his gaze to the peepal tree beside him and its sprawling branches, and said to Raghavan, "Brother, what an impressive tree it is! Its branches cover the entire area with fruits everywhere yet see! Is there a cuckoo or sparrow in the tree?" Raghavan wondered to himself when he noticed there were no birds in the large tree, 'why don't birds come to this tree?' With that thought in mind, he looked at Malaimayan.

Malaimayan inquired once more, "Do you have any clue what led to it?" This was his following question. Raghavan shook his head, appearing equally uninformed, and allowed him to provide an explanation. However, Malaimayan quickly said, "I don't have a clue either!" Then he gazed at Raghavan, who was perplexed by these queries, and stated philosophically, "Brother! Many things in life are beyond explanation. Occasionally, you just need to accept circumstances as they are."

Malaimayan began abruptly, "Raghava! Right here between us is where your father Devanathan's lifeless body was discovered. He was positioned with his upper body on the stone platform and his lower body on these stairs. His death was peculiar as there were no injuries on him." He then paused and admitted, "To some extent, I am to blame for your father's demise," while examining Raghavan's face intently.

Raghavan wasn't surprised by what Malaimayan shared. He was lost in thought. He had received different information from Manikandan. Malaimayan, on the other hand, had another story to tell. Convinced there was a mystery surrounding his father's death, Raghavan turned to Malaimayan and said, "Grandfather! I'm having trouble understanding, could you explain further?" Malaimayan replied, "Even if you hadn't asked, there would come a time for me to reveal it. Today, I will share everything," as he began recounting the old sorrowful events.

Malaimayan discarded the cigar and began recounting the past occurrences just as he had done twice before with Raghavan. His mind was overwhelmed with memories. Yet, as expected, he spoke with a stammer, while Raghavan absorbed these fragmented thoughts and grasped their complete meaning. The tale resumed precisely where it had paused earlier at the lakeshore.

Alan Williams was in a profound daze when Mayan arrived at the lake's edge after bringing assistance. The crocodile's bitten leg was still bleeding. Much blood had been lost. The rescuers quickly wrapped cloth around Alan Williams's leg and swiftly carried him to the mansion. He instructed four men to transport the deceased leopard from the boat to the hunting mansion and then followed behind Alan Williams. From the mansion, Alan Williams was hurried to the hill town hospital.

Following a month of medical care, Alan Williams was taken from the hospital to the hunting mansion, where his treatment persisted. Arrangements were made for a doctor and an assistant to visit daily to monitor his condition. While he refrained from inquiring about Soman during his hospital stay, once at the hunting mansion, Alan Williams began questioning everyone about Soman's fate.

One day, he inquired to Mayan regarding Soman, and Mayan began to cry bitterly as he recounted what had occurred to Soman by the lakefront. Alan Williams shook with emotion upon receiving the news. Overcome by the loss of Soman, he began to weep. Mayan found it difficult to handle Alan Williams, who was lying on the bed, sobbing uncontrollably for Soman.

Alan Williams's health began to decline from the moment he learned about Soman's tragic passing. Alan felt he was to blame for this death. Mayan was regretful that he couldn't console Williams. After six months, his health still hadn't improved. As usual, one morning Mayan went to check on Alan Williams and was taken aback! Alan was awkwardly standing right beneath the statue of the goddess on the mansion's reception hall floor.

Mayan hurried over, astonished to see the man who hadn't been able to get out of bed for half a year now standing upright. Alan halted him at his side and remarked how glad he was that Mayan had arrived. Indicating the Amman statue, he said, "Mayan! observe the red stone in the goddess's crown, it isn't just a beautiful stone! It's a valuable ruby. An invaluable antique. It must remain there. Don't let anyone else have it." The man stood gazing at the goddess for some time. Suddenly, his body collapsed forward like a felled tree, bowing before the Goddess. Alarmed, Mayan approached to check on him. Alan Williams had passed away.

As Alan Williams's existence vanished, a significant secret was unveiled to Mayan. Rising to his feet, Mayan gazed at the statue of Amman. The light from an unknown source caused the Ruby stone embedded in the crown to glitter in Mayan's eyes.

Chapter 17

Devanathan's Fate

After the tragic loss of Soman, followed by the death of Alan Williams, significant alterations occurred within the tea estate and mill. Soman's son, Devanathan, who had finished his education, was assigned a crucial role in the tea factory and became part of its management team. Mayan's life, however, remained largely unchanged, as he continued to reside with his wife in the hunting mansion.

The couple preserved the mansion exactly as it had been during Alan Williams' lifetime. However, stories about the hunting mansion circulated, and no one was willing to take up residence there. The local inhabitants steered clear of even approaching the hunting mansion, as they thought a force was present there and avoided provoking its anger by venturing there without reason.

Alan Williams, who oversaw the planning and construction of every part of the mansion, passed away before having much time to enjoy it. Mayan and his wife were the only residents of the large hunting mansion, which was both beautiful and frightening. Despite circulating rumours, they remained safe. However, tragedy struck when Mayan's wife unexpectedly fell ill and died, leaving Mayan by himself in the mansion.

Even though he maintained his duties in that grand estate, his confidence in moving through the mansion was not as strong as it once was. Having his wife by his side provided him with strength and bravery. Her passing diminished him even more. He was left with no option but to remain living there. Consequently, he adopted a new habit within a short time.

He cut his wife's saree into long strips and wrapped them around his right arm just below the elbow in different colours. He placed his wife's bracelets on his left hand in that spot. Furthermore, he tied his wife's wedding badge string around his right ankle and attached one of her silver anklets to his left leg. He also applied a one-inch-wide saffron mark on his forehead. These elements combined to make Mayan appear even more intimidating. Following that, the local people avoided him. He walked around shirtless, wearing a black dhoti at his waist. He believed these items gave him a sense of his wife's presence, allowing him to carry out his daily tasks peacefully.

Malaimayan had moved past his old memories. He revealed to Raghavan the unusual items on his hands and legs. Noticing that Malaimayan hadn't abandoned that habit for nearly thirty-five years, Raghavan stared at him in astonishment. Malaimayan went on, "At that time, your father Devanathan was already grown up. Before long, he mastered all the tasks at the tea factory and earned everyone's respect. A few years later, he met a woman and married her. You were born within a year. Unfortunately, your father's bad luck mirrored your grandfather's. Like Soman's wife, your mother passed away during childbirth. Devanathan took on the responsibility of raising you. He nurtured you well. Yet, oddly, his fate was sealed in a single day." With that, he fell silent and lowered his head.

After some time, Raghavan glanced at Malaimayan, who had his head bowed in guilt. "Grandfather! Don't fret over past events. Whatever your mistake in that was, I won't consider it serious. Please tell me exactly what transpired," he urged. Encouraged by Raghavan, Malaimayan began to recount his old memories once more. He noticed Raghavan sitting on the stone stage and folded his legs as he sat down, before continuing the rest of the story.

Mayan lived according to his own style, managing the hunting estate. However, he carried a significant burden in his thoughts. It began to show each day whenever he looked at the goddess statue in the mansion. Due to his declining health, he resolved to disclose the secret he had kept in his mind to the right person as soon as he could. He selected Devanathan for this task. His choice was sound, yet he hadn't considered that it would impact Devanathan's destiny.

One afternoon, Mayan arrived at the hunting mansion alongside Devanathan. Initially, he guided Devanathan through the mansion, as Devanathan had never ventured there before that day. Devanathan was both unsettled by the mansion's magnificent beauty and its underlying dread. Within the mansion, Mayan eventually positioned him before the goddess statue located in the reception room. Devanathan stood in the exact spot where Alan Williams had stood several years earlier.

Mayan revealed the goddess statue's crown to him and started explaining the reality of the diamond embedded in it. From that point, destiny began its play. The play commenced in a toddy shop in the hill town roughly fifteen kilometres away.

An elderly man was sipping toddy in the shop that afternoon. The clay pot in front of him was empty. He summoned the shop worker, demanding another drink with an authoritative tone. The waiter approached and remarked, "Listen, old man...! You haven't paid for your last drink, and now you're asking for more. I can't explain this to my boss. Pay up," the waiter responded firmly.

The inebriated old man began to grow irate and declared, "You young lad, you don't know anything about me. Are you aware that I'm a millionaire, even just thinking about it now?" Observing the old man, the waiter chuckled and replied, "Yes... you are a wealth hoarder, to pour in crores of money..." and proceeded to ignore him. The old man attempted to rise in his anger but ended up falling to the ground. He grabbed hold of the shop attendant to help himself back up and said, "Hey, I'm drunk, but I speak only the truth. There's treasure...! It's right here...!" He pounded his chest repeatedly. He leaned against the boy in his drunken state, murmuring, "A secret of sixty years..., if I reveal it, you too could become a millionaire."

The shop boy sensed that the old man might be hiding something. Without delay, he left the old man resting against the wall and fetched some water and toddy. He splashed water on the old man's face to rouse him and handed him the toddy. Carelessly, the old man revealed the secret to the boy.

In the hunting mansion, Mayan remarked, "The statue has been taken off the pedestal."

The elderly man at the toddy shop lamented, "The trident has been detached from the statue."

"A stone from the crown cracked and fell onto the stage," noted Mayan.

"I witnessed it fall," added the old man.

"Williams considered it just an ordinary stone," mentioned Mayan.

"I realized it was a precious gem," the old man admitted.

"Williams pocketed the stone and departed," recounted Mayan.

"He took me with him," said the old man.

"Even after discovering it was a diamond, he restored it to the statue with a carpenter's help," Mayan explained.

"I was that carpenter," the old man said.

"This secret is known only to us," Mayan revealed to Devanathan.

"The statue remains at the hunting mansion," the old man told the boy, concluding his tale. Subsequently, the boy silenced the old man.

The details shared by Mayan were unfamiliar to Devanathan. He pondered, 'The stone is inside the statue, which is in the hunting mansion, and Mayan is at home for protection. Why is there this unnecessary issue? Is there any reason to get involved?' Deciding he could discuss it later; he proceeded to his job.

The following day at midday, Devanathan arrived at the hunting mansion to see Mayan. As he got closer to the mansion, he heard 'thud…', 'thud…' sound from inside and assumed that Mayan was engaged in some work, prompting him to proceed to the mansion's entrance. He was taken aback by what he saw. A young man, probably in his early twenties, had climbed onto the statue, balancing one leg on the hands holding the goddess's Trident, attempting to pry out a red diamond set into the crown.

Overtaken by fury, Devanathan yelled, "Hey… who… is that…!" He continued to shout, "Thief…! Thief…!" The man fixated on the stone abruptly glanced towards the source of the commotion. At that moment, his sharp tool fully detached the diamond, causing it to spring from the crown and drop.

Observing the stone that had descended right before him, he readied himself to climb down from the statue and began descending to retrieve the stone. The crimson diamond that dropped to the reception hall floor rolled and came to rest at Devanathan's feet as he stood in the doorway, yelling.

Recognizing what it was, Devanathan crouched, placed it in his pocket, and yelled, "Mayan…! Mayan…! Quick, there's a thief!" As he shouted, he moved to call Mayan. At that moment, the thief descended from the first floor and lunged at Devanathan with a sharp instrument in his grip.

By the time Devanathan faced Mayan's house, the thief tripped and fell on the doorstep. His weapon slipped from his grasp, vanishing into the dense foliage near the mansion's entrance. Hearing the commotion, Mayan rushed out of his house but was confused about the situation. Just as Mayan reached the scene, Devanathan pivoted towards the door to apprehend the thief. However, the thief, now back on his feet, spotted two men approaching and bolted around to the rear of the mansion.

Devanathan, accompanied by Mayan, tracked the thief to the rear of the mansion to look for him, but the thief vanished. Still confused, Mayan, who was with Devanathan, inquired about the situation. Devanathan signalled for silence as he scanned the surroundings. When the thief was nowhere to be seen, Devanathan took hold of Mayan's hand and headed towards the mansion's entrance.

In the mansion's reception area, he presented the idol of the Goddess to Mayan. "Where is the stone?" Mayan asked, astonished by its absence. Devanathan retrieved the stone from his pocket and handed it to Mayan. "Mayan, someone else is aware of this stone's secret. We need to find who attempted to steal it." With that, he continued to explain to Mayan everything that had transpired.

Overwhelmed with shock and fear, Mayan held the diamond in his palm and shook. As they both gazed at the gem, it emitted beams of light, casting a blood-red hue on their already anxious, pale faces.

Devanathan, having quickly reached a decision, turned to Mayan, and shared his thoughts. "Mayan! Conceal it in a secure location at once. Afterwards, we can consider attaching it to the idol and safeguarding it. I am departing to search for the thief once more." With that, he exited the mansion.

Devanathan returned to the mansion's rear and began exploring. He wandered through the trees surrounding the mansion, searching for any sign of the thief. Despite his efforts, he saw nothing. Ultimately, he deduced that the thief had fled in fright. He headed towards his home, believing it was unnecessary to return to the mansion. Unbeknownst to him, the thief was concealed in Mayan's house.

The burglar inside Mayan's home observed through the outhouse window as Devanathan began his walk toward the stone platform. After Devanathan passed through the wooded area encircling the mansion and stepped into the tea garden, the burglar exited Mayan's home and discreetly trailed Devanathan, staying concealed among the trees and foliage.

The moment Devanathan exited the mansion, Mayan found himself holding the red diamond, uncertain of where to conceal it. As he scanned the reception room, no spot appeared suitable. At that moment, through the hall window, he noticed someone was tailing Devanathan.

Feeling anxious with the threat on his mind, he knew he had to act swiftly. Holding the diamond, he understood it needed to be concealed right away. He dashed to the animal hall. Upon entering, he noticed a collection of animal skins he had gathered to craft animal toys, and beside it, a container full of glass shards, nails, and teeth. Without hesitation, he opened the container and mingled the diamond with the glass beads inside. He then shut the container, placed it among the heap of skins, and hurriedly ran towards the thief pursuing Devanathan.

Devanathan arrived at the distant peepal tree before Mayan had crossed the mansion's boundary and entered the tea garden. The thief following him was trailing twenty feet behind, hidden among the tea plants.

Moments after Devanathan descended to the stone stage beneath the peepal tree, Mayan noticed the thief attacking Devanathan. Mayan had just arrived at the tea garden. Observing from a distance, he saw the thief shove Devanathan forward, sit on him, and choke him. Mayan dashed towards the stone stage, screaming, but his cries disappeared into the air.

Upon arriving at the base of the stone stage, Mayan was shocked by the sight before him. The thief had attacked Devanathan on the stone stage. Devanathan's body was partly slumped on the platform and partly on the steps, as he gazed at the peepal tree's branches above, with no movement in his form.

The burglar anxiously searched for the diamond in his pockets and pants. He failed to notice Mayan sneaking up on him from the rear. Mayan grabbed a dark stone from the ground and leapt onto the burglar. With equal swiftness, he lifted the rock in his hand above the thief's head and slammed it down with rage. The impact likely fractured his skull; however, the stone descended, grazing the rear of the right side and ripping the skin.

Startled by the unexpected hit to his head, he touched the spot where the impact occurred and looked back. Spotting an emaciated man holding a rock in his hand, he angrily reached out and kicked Mayan. The blow from the thief's foot landed hard on Mayan's chest. Unable to block the kick, Mayan staggered backward four steps and collapsed.

The thief removed his hand from his head and was shocked to discover it was stained with blood. Blood was also trickling from his head down his cheek. Acknowledging that he was unable to manage the situation, the thief began to flee. He quickly slipped into the bushes behind the stone stage and escaped within a few minutes.

Mayan, writhing under the peepal tree from the pain of the kick, got to his feet unsteadily. He flung the stone stage he was clutching into the bushes and approached Devanathan to rouse him. As Devanathan lay inert, the man who contacted his body flinched and drew back in surprise.

Mayan trembled as he realized Devanathan was dead. He stumbled backward, collapsing onto the spot where he'd been kicked to the ground. He covered his face with his hands, paralyzed and unsure of his next move.

Malaimayan sat across from Raghavan as he had beneath the peepal tree that day, his face buried in his hands. His body trembled subtly, yet tears did not fall from his eyes. The impact of witnessing the third death up close was still etched on his face.

Raghavan, standing before him, was stunned by the circumstances surrounding his father's death. After a few minutes of silence among those present, Malaimayan was the first to break it, saying, "Brother, the turn of events that began on the afternoon of the first day concluded by the afternoon of the following day. In merely a day. I was the cause." With tears in his eyes, Malaimayan implored Raghavan, "Forgive me, brother."

Raghavan gazed at it in silence. Gradually, he rose from the stone platform and began to make his way home, leaning on his crutch. Malaimayan, seated on the stone platform with eyes full of worry, watched as Raghavan's figure slowly faded behind a curtain of tears.

Chapter 18

Saru Again

It was one of the rare times of the year when the weather was favourable. The temperature was mild, without an excessive cold that could send shivers through the body. Although the sun radiated brightly, its warmth wasn't overpowering, as the refreshing breeze helped mitigate its effects. In this agreeable setting, Raghavan rose from the stone platform and began his walk home, having just heard the devastating news of his father's violent demise.

Raghavan departed from the stone stage area and stepped into the tea plantation. Despite the agreeable climate, he found himself perspiring. The confirmed news of his father's passing had deeply disturbed him. The reality was surprisingly different from the swirling rumours. He contemplated this disparity as he made his way back home

Since then, he had isolated himself at home for several days. Thoughts of his father's tragic demise repeatedly haunted him. He struggled to accept that his father's joyful life had abruptly ended in a single day. Who was to blame for this? Was it the person who killed his father and fled? Or was it Malaimayan, who was admitting something? Or was it his father, who unwisely got involved and lost his life? Ultimately, was the diamond that was at the centre of all these events to blame? After pondering deeply, he could not arrive at any conclusion.

He couldn't comprehend one aspect. If his father was indeed killed for a diamond, then how did the story circulate that his death was caused by God's wrath and that Soolamuni's fury led to his demise? He partially uncovered the answer from Manikandan.

Devanathan was discovered after disappearing at the tea factory that afternoon. Several hours had passed since his death, and his body had been placed before Soolamuni on the stone platform. Upon learning of the situation, Manikandan promptly went there. Only Devanathan's body remained, as Malaimayan had already departed.

In an instant, a small crowd formed. The assembled group began discussing Devanathan's untimely demise with Soolamuni, concocting a false story by the time law enforcement arrived. During the police interrogation, Manikandan observed Malaimayan arriving from some direction and joining the crowd. Malaimayan aligned himself with the crowd, endorsing the account fabricated by the people there. Everyone present relayed the same story to the police. However, the police remained skeptical of the tale, yet they found no additional clues.

Once the authorities removed Devanathan's body, the crowd gradually thinned out until only Manikandan and Malaimayan remained by the stone stage. Malaimayan moved toward Manikandan to speak, but Manikandan backed away, refusing to engage in conversation. Malaimayan reconsidered and retraced his steps. Left alone, Manikandan quickly exited the area, driven by fear.

Raghavan was notified, although he was at a great distance. Since it would take him over three days to arrive, Manikandan had to conduct the formal rituals in Raghavan's stead. Malaimayan took part in all the ceremonies. Following the completion of the formalities, Malaimayan visited Manikandan's shop and shared some new information with him.

Once Malaimayan inquired Manikandan about the specifics of 'when will Raghavan arrive? and when will he depart?' he began recounting the tale of Soolamuni, who came to the stone stage at noon each day to smoke a cigar. His account resembled what those gathered around Devanathan's corpse had said on that occasion. Manikandan took this as true. That was the message Manikandan relayed to Raghavan to caution him. Following the cigar tale, he urged Manikandan to leave a cigar on the stone stage before the Trident daily from that point forward to validate his story. Manikandan followed this practice routinely.

After gathering numerous details from Manikandan, Raghavan contemplated the information and found himself astonished. It became clear how Malaimayan turned the murder into a crime of the deity. But for what reason? Several thoughts occurred as he pondered over it. Malaimayan was the sole individual at the murder site. Thus, he realized there was a strong likelihood that the murder accusation would be directed at him, and he employed that narrative as a cover-up. In addition, Malaimayan was accomplishing something significant at the same time.

Raghavan realized that Malaimayan had managed to keep the red diamond's secret hidden by attributing the incident to the deity. Only three individuals were aware of the diamond's secret. The owner of the diamond was Malaimayan, while the other two were simply privy to it. One of these two was attempting to steal the diamond, and the third individual was Raghavan.

Raghavan recalled the day his father discovered the diamond and acted, which unfortunately led to a tragic end to his father's life. Consequently, he determined that from then on, he would refrain from getting involved in any issues concerning the diamond. Supporting his decision, Malaimayan also approached him a few days later and made a promise.

Within a week after Malaimayan met Raghavan at the stone stage, Malaimayan visited Raghavan's home looking for him. As soon as he arrived, he immediately spoke to Raghavan, delivered his message, and left quickly.

"Raghava, my brother! I possess that red stone. If I'm around, you are safe from harm. Following your father's instructions, I've concealed it securely where nobody can discover it." With determination, he assured Raghavan, "I will reveal its secret location to you before my death!" After mentioning this with some tension, he departed, stating that his purpose there had been fulfilled.

Malaimayan's words were completely understood by him. Even though he mentioned that a significant burden would be placed on him, he felt somewhat relieved at that moment. As determined days prior, he could focus solely on his tasks. He realized that with Malaimayan's presence, there would be no issues.

Malaimayan's reassuring words provided significant comfort to Raghavan. As he pondered his next steps, Poonkuzhali arrived to offer him a task. That evening, she returned from school and dashed to Raghavan's place with documents in hand, resembling a swift sparrow. Upon entering, she presented the papers to Raghavan. He carefully reviewed each one and gazed at Poonkuzhali with pride. What he observed were her graded answer sheets from the annual exams, in which Poonkuzhali achieved perfect scores in every subject.

He enthusiastically complimented her achievements in the first grade and suggested that she should demonstrate her abilities in future classes as well. She mentioned, "school is closed for two months." While he was pondering his next steps, she came up with the answer. He promptly decided that he could impart some of his knowledge to the child over the two-month break. "Take the papers home and show them to both your mom and dad." He sent her off with the assurance, "I will visit home tomorrow."

The following morning, as Manikandan was heading to her house, he remembered to bring the boxes of picture puzzles he had purchased for Poonkuzhali as a gift. Poonkuzhali was seated at the entrance when he arrived at the street. Upon seeing Raghavan approach, she immediately jumped up and ran to him. He handed her the two boxes. She accompanied him, examining every side of the boxes, unaware of what they contained. Once they arrived at the door, they both sat down on the doorstep. Meanwhile, Manikandan went to the shop, and Chitra headed to the tea factory.

Raghavan began by unlocking the simplest puzzle box he had with him, removed a picture from inside, laid it out on the step, and instructed on assembling the puzzle pieces, which had been carved into various shapes. He then instructed that the remaining four puzzles in the box be completed in the same manner and approached the children playing nearby. Within a short time, he identified which of them ought to be admitted to the school for the upcoming academic year and went back to Poonkuzhali.

The four puzzle pictures he had placed on the doorstep were finished. Poonkuzhali pointed out the house's floor to him. There lay the box containing the challenging puzzles, opened, and she had also completed the five puzzle pictures. Expecting the simple puzzles to take ten minutes and the complex ones at least thirty minutes, he was amazed that she completed all of them in ten minutes. Recognizing her unique abilities, he broke apart the puzzle pictures and asked her to solve them again before heading back home.

The following day, Raghavan travelled to the city at the bottom of the hill where he purchased toys and books for Poonkuzhali. Later that evening, in the presence of Manikandan and Chitra, he presented Poonkuzhali with the items and suggested ways for her to enjoy her vacation. Poonkuzhali's joy was evident on her face. However, Chitra was concerned about the lack of storage space for those items at home.

Raghavan provided a solution. He cleared out a wooden cupboard in his house and moved it to the front room to hold books. He filled it with all his purchased items and allowed Poonkuzhali to go home for meals and rest, returning during other times to be productive. He also mentioned that other children were welcome to join her in play. He assigned Poonkuzhali the responsibility of looking after all the items. This setup was well-received by everyone. In a matter of days, the front room of his house became bustling with activity during the day.

The boys primarily engaged themselves with the carrom board. Raghavan purchased a 'Rubik's' cube for Poonkuzhali. Expecting her to pick it up when she wished, he started introducing and teaching her how to play chess. Poonkuzhali was thrilled with excitement. Just like the boys, Raghavan also found joy in his days.

Poonkuzhali enjoyed reading books and playing carrom with the boys, as well as playing chess with Raghavan. Even when the boys didn't show up, she always attended. One day, Raghavan was instructing her on some important endgame strategies in chess. Abruptly, Poonkuzhali's focus shifted, and she started listening intently to a noise emanating from the backyard.

Raghavan was unable to hear anything. He glanced at Poonkuzhali, who rose and eagerly exclaimed, "Uncle... Saru, Uncle..." while pointing towards the backyard. Despite this, Raghavan was still puzzled by Poonkuzhali's behaviour. As he observed, she hurried to the backyard. Raghavan picked up the crutch and went after her. The sight before him was astonishing.

Under the fig tree, Poonkuzhali stood with a radiantly bright face. Saru was perched on her right shoulder. Raghavan felt as though the Goddess Meenakshi Amman appeared as a child at that moment, with Poonkuzhali wearing a green skirt and shirt along with a parrot on her shoulder. He lost himself in the moment. Raghavan came back to reality upon hearing Saru's call of 'kee… kee… kee… kee….' He joyfully stretched out his left hand towards Saru. Saru flew over and perched right onto his extended hand, calling out to Poonkuzhali, 'kee… kee… kee… kee…'

Raghavan and Saru entered the house together without Saru showing any hesitation. Poonkuzhali transformed into a butterfly and flew to Manikandan's shop, returning with a paper bag full of millet mixture. Saru alternated glances between them and nibbled on the millets in Poonkuzhali's hands. Overjoyed by this, the two of them began conversing with Saru. However, Saru only replied with a 'kee… kee… kee…' and suddenly spoke two words that delighted them: 'Come… ok… ok… kee… kee… kee…' These were words often said by Raghavan and Poonkuzhali around Saru. Instantly, Saru took off from their hand and flew to the backyard.

The people who were momentarily shocked by Saru's speech hurried to the backyard in dismay. When they arrived, they saw Saru soaring into the distance. They stood for a long time staring in the direction Saru had flown, hoping for a return. Entering the house with a sense of sadness, there was no other activity to engage in that day. The joy Saru had given them never faded.

Their hopes were justified as Saru returned to that place after a few days. Its visits increased in frequency afterward. On one occasion, Saru arrived with a tiny lump of clay in its mouth and then departed. The clay was as small as a pea. Why? Why? Raghavan was taken aback. Unable to understand the reasons, he placed it securely in a small box, considering it a gift from Saru.

The start of the second grade coincided with the end of Poonkuzhali's vacation. Raghavan registered two additional boys in the school. Poonkuzhali excelled in her academics as well as in co-curricular and extracurricular activities. She consistently ranked first in all her classes. She was emerging as a highly talented girl who enjoyed reading numerous books and acquiring new skills during each vacation. As the years went by, she continued to grow and develop.

It was the first day of her 11th grade. Raghavan was over the age of forty-five. She opted for History and Sociology in her senior secondary education. Raghavan stood by the door, ready to see Poonkuzhali off to school.

From afar, he noticed Poonkuzhali approaching, dressed differently than usual. Chitra accompanied her. As she drew nearer, he observed that Poonkuzhali appeared stunning. Her hair was styled in a double braid, and she wore a churidar with a dupatta. With her forehead adorned with small sandalwood and saffron marks, she smiled warmly at Raghavan and greeted him, "Good morning… uncle." He responded in kind and instructed, "You take the bus. I'll follow later." He added, "We need to arrange for your hostel admission." After replying "Okay uncle," she and Chitra proceeded to Manikandan's shop.

The moment Poonkuzhali got on the bus, Raghavan glanced at Manikandan and Chitra and remarked, "Kuzhali has matured." Chitra responded with joy and excitement, "Yes, brother." However, Manikandan appeared slightly concerned. Even though he took great pride in his daughter's development, there was an unspoken concern he held. Raghavan approached him, reassuringly patted his shoulder, and advised him not to worry since he was there for him, then headed back home.

He completed his morning tasks and prepared to head to school. Poonkuzhali needed to purchase textbooks, notebooks, and other essentials. Additionally, she had to be enrolled in the hostel. He opened the wooden cabinet to retrieve money for these purposes. Upon noticing the tin box, he picked it up and opened it to find small clumps of clay, which Saru had brought periodically. The box was nearly full, and he couldn't discern its purpose. Saru continued to make those contributions. However, little did he realize that it would eventually be of significant assistance to him. He shut the box and departed with the cash.

Chapter 19

Radhika Teacher

At eleven in the morning, Raghavan arrived at Poonkuzhali's school. It was the first day after the break, and no classes were conducted. He willingly took Poonkuzhali to purchase her required textbooks.

The clouds looked ominous, suggesting that rain was imminent. He quickly took Poonkuzhali to the store to purchase everything before the rainfall began. Once they had acquired all the goods as per the list provided by the school, they headed back to the school. The rain began to pour down. Unable to traverse the playground to reach the hostel, they waited under the veranda for the rain to cease.

During that moment, Poonkuzhali noticed a teacher walking by carrying some books. She acknowledged her with a salute and stepped aside. The teacher looked over and gave both her and Raghavan, who was nearby, a warm smile in greeting. After the teacher departed, Poonkuzhali remarked, "That's Radhika teacher, my 10th-grade teacher." Raghavan nodded; his attention fixed on waiting for the rain to cease.

Eventually, the rain ceased. However, the hostel tasks had to wait until after lunch as the break buzzer had sounded. Poonkuzhali invited Raghavan to sit beside her on a cement bench near the playground, which she had dried of raindrops. She opened her lunch container, placed some food in the lid, and offered it to Raghavan, while she began eating the remainder.

As they were having their meal, Teacher Radhika arrived to find them. The newcomer took a seat beside Poonkuzhali and opened her lunchbox. She set aside two spoonsful of curd rice for Poonkuzhali and Raghavan and then began her meal. While eating, she mentioned with a smile, "I teach Poonkuzhali in class 10. I also teach the same class in the eleventh grade and continue in the twelfth."

"Poonkuzhali is an outstanding student and a great asset to our school," she remarked while glancing at Raghavan. Raghavan, unsure of what to say, looked back at her. She went on, "She not only excels academically, but also shines in extra-curricular activities!" Despite being aware of this, Raghavan listened attentively. "I will ensure that Poonkuzhali is taken care of. That's my duty. If you're heading home, it seems like it might rain again," she added."

Raghavan cut her off, stating, "Poonkuzhali needs to be enrolled in the hostel, but it can only be arranged after the lunch break," he paused. She immediately became enthusiastic and replied, "As the hostel warden, let's proceed and get it done. I'm also in charge of her there," she chuckled. The three of them completed their meal, and within the following hour, Raghavan departed for home after finalizing the hostel enrolment.

"Visit your daughter frequently," Radhika said, glancing at Raghavan. Poonkuzhali remarked, "Goodbye uncle." Radhika abruptly turned to Poonkuzhali in surprise. Raghavan walked away grinning when he saw that reaction.

The following week was dedicated to addressing the hostel needs for Poonkuzhali. Completing the tasks proved challenging due to the relentless rain. Once settled in the hostel, she was able to pursue her education without breaks, regardless of the weather conditions like rain, snow, or cold. Teacher Radhika was also present to support her. He concluded that there should be no issues until Poonkuzhali finishes her higher secondary education. However, he decided to visit the school at least once a month to check on Poonkuzhali's progress in her studies.

Following his plan, Raghavan visited the school the following month to ask about Poonkuzhali. The school permitted parents or relatives to meet with students only during the lunch break. Raghavan waited outside until the bell signalled lunch break before entering. Poonkuzhali was not present in the classroom. She had gone to the hostel for lunch. Radhika teacher escorted him to the hostel.

She had Raghavan remain in her room until Poonghuzhali completed her meal, after which she brought Poongkuzhali in and permitted them to converse. Later, she indicated that it was nearly time for classes to commence and instructed Poonghuzhali to attend her class. She then opened her lunchbox, prepared to eat, placed some food on the lid for Raghavan, and began her meal without paying attention to him.

While eating, Teacher Radhika remarked, "Poonkuzhali mentioned you're a friend of her father..." Raghavan grinned and replied, "Yes, teacher, Poonkuzhali's father and I are very good friends. There was an event, which is why he couldn't attend. Even her mother couldn't." He paused and added, "Also, I am currently without employment." Glancing at the teacher, Raghavan continued, "I retired after my time in the army," raising his crutch high. Without waiting for another query, he motioned to his left leg, explaining, "A decade ago, a bomb blast impaired my leg."

Radhika's expression shifted slightly in response to his words, and although she quickly concealed it, Raghavan caught the change. The teacher wrapped up by mentioning she also needed to attend her class. He went back home. Over the months that ensued, they kept meeting, and a friendship flourished between them.

During the meeting, Radhika unexpectedly asked about Raghavan's wife. "What is your wife's name?" Caught off guard and not even considering mentioning that he was single, he blurted out the first name that came to mind: Saru. "Does Saru stand for Sarumati? Sarulata? Or maybe Saruprabha?" Ms. Radhika asked persistently. Observing her insistence, he simply replied, "No, it's just Saru."

Yet Radhika persisted and consistently made it a point to ask about Saru in every following meeting. He struggled to handle this. However, during a conversation about Saru with Poonkuzhali, Raghavan's act was disclosed to her. She discovered that Saru was a parrot that frequently visited Raghavan's home. Poonkuzhali provided her with all the details. Radhika was moved by Raghavan's bond and fondness for the parrot. She found enjoyment in Raghavan's charade and decided to proceed with it. Her choice began to manifest in future meetings and caused issues for Raghavan.

Through Poonkuzhali, she learned everything about Raghavan and felt a certain sympathy for him. Eagerly anticipating the day they would meet, Radhika expressed to Raghavan in their subsequent encounter that it was right to refer to her as 'Radhika' and inquired, "I would like to meet your wife." She took pleasure in Raghavan's flustered reaction to her unexpected query, "Why not? Can I meet Saru, or will you bring her here?" she pressed. He quickly responded, "No... no... don't, she won't come. You can visit when I let you know," as he contemplated Saru's reaction. He wasn't sure how much longer he could withstand the pressure. Her following question only intensified the situation.

"What does Saru look like?" As he thought about how to respond to Radhika's inquiry, she went on, "Does she appear lovely like a parrot?" He replied, stuttering, "Yes, like a parrot." He expected her to go away, disappointedly. However, Radhika persisted. "Describe Saru's way of speaking. Is it as delightful as a parrot's chatter?" He gazed at her with suspicion. She maintained an innocent expression and added, "No... I just asked because Saru is as charming as a parrot." She watched his face for his reaction. He then stated briefly, "Yes, she speaks like a parrot. She doesn't say much," and concluded, "Alright, I'm on my way. Let's meet again."

Radhika was determined not to let him leave like that. "Wait, I'm coming with you. I must meet Saru today," she insisted firmly. The situation became very distressing for Raghavan, yet he managed to endure it. "No need to rush," he replied. "I'll tell Saru about you first, then I'll bring you to her. She might be frightened if she unexpectedly encounters strangers." Raghavan halted Radhika and stepped away. After leaving, he resolved never to see the teacher again.

As events unfolded, Raghavan was not required to see the teacher for a few upcoming months. Shortly after, Poonkuzhali returned home for a vacation following her yearly exams.

During the holidays, his house became lively as usual. All the children, who previously played at the workers' residences, were now attending school together. Thus, they would meet daily at his house, accompanied by Poonkuzhali. Raghavan had set up a modest library in the front room.

In addition to sports facilities, the library's collection of books allowed the students to enjoy their holidays. Furthermore, Raghavan began offering them lessons in essay writing and oratory skills. Poonkuzhali did not require his instruction since she had acquired significant talent at school. Therefore, she no longer needs Raghavan as an instructor. During the holidays, Raghavan understood that she required an exceptional coach to help her progress further.

Once the vacation ended and the students returned to school, Raghavan's house was empty once more. As Poonkuzhali started twelfth grade, Raghavan saw no need to ask about her studies, which also allowed him to avoid meeting Radhika. He planned to meet her before Poonkuzhali's yearly exams to talk about her higher education. However, he had another task to complete first.

Over the years, Raghavan had lost touch with Malaimayan. Recently, during a visit to Manikandan's store, Manikandan mentioned that Malaimayan no longer comes to get cigars from him. Raghavan understood why; it was a secret shared only between him and Malaimayan. He felt that Malaimayan seemed to have abandoned the tale of Soolamuni, as if it was no longer significant. Many years had passed since he last saw Malaimayan, and he grew concerned about his health, prompting him to decide to visit Malaimayan.

On a day in the month preceding heavy snowfall, Raghavan set out to visit Malaimayan. The tea garden's ambiance was pleasant. Although unpleasant memories from the past arose as he passed the stone stage area, he swiftly moved past it, entered the subsequent tea garden, and approached the hunting mansion. Upon reaching Malaimayan's house, he peered inside but found him absent. Raghavan concluded that he might be in the hunting mansion and proceeded to its door. It was Raghavan's first time entering the hunting mansion. The mansion's doors stood open.

Chapter 20

Hunting Mansion

As Raghavan stood at the entrance of the hunting mansion, he could not clearly see what was inside for a moment. The mansion was somewhat dim even during daylight hours. No lamps were installed for lighting. Aside from the overhead light entering through the door, the illumination from the two windows flanking the front reception room revealed the look of the front hall.

Raghavan descended from the steps to the floor of the reception area and moved slightly forward. In the room's dim light, the arrangement and contents became more discernible. The first thing that drew his attention was the statue of Amman, positioned on the edge of the upstairs veranda overlooking the lower front room. Raghavan paused for a few moments, staring at the bright face of Amman, who was situated at the centre of the mansion, clutching a Trident in her right hand. Aside from the goddess statue, all other items in the room appeared frightening.

Wide staircases situated on each side of the chamber bordered the windows on both ends and ascended in a curve to reach the upper veranda. The wooden columns and the stairway handrails featured carvings of different animals and birds, showcasing both elegance and intimidation.

The back section of the reception area was covered by the terraced veranda. Raghavan observed the walls of the front room, which were adorned with different animal heads. Deer heads with horns spaced at varying distances. Bison heads had curved horns extending from each side of the head, meeting in the middle. Elephant heads were complete with tusks. In certain spots, iguanas were depicted as if crawling up the walls in full form. Everything was crafted with such realism that the animals appeared almost alive. The eyes of every animal mounted on the wall resembled those of fierce creatures, seemingly staring intently at Raghavan, who stood on the ground floor, causing him to shudder. Even the deer heads instilled some fear in him.

Raghavan gazed down from the veranda above. There were two rooms on either side, each with their doors shut. Directly across from his position, a doorless entryway resembling a main doorway revealed a dark room. Since Malaimayan was not visible, Raghavan proceeded toward the gloomy room in search of him. As Raghavan neared the entrance of the dark room, Malaimayan emerged from within. Raghavan halted in shock as Malaimayan rushed out, resembling a living skeleton.

Malaimayan, having emerged upon hearing the bustle, was surprised to see Raghavan standing before him. He held wooden sticks with brush-like tips of various sizes and a small broom in his hands.

It appeared he was tidying up the area. Raghavan explained to Malaimayan why he had arrived and paused there. Malaimayan nodded with a smile and said, "Alright, let's go explore the mansion," inviting Raghavan. Raghavan pointed out the front reception area and remarked, "I've seen this." "In that case, follow me...! This hall is the marvel of the mansion." He guided Raghavan into the dim room from which he had emerged.

Even though he was eager to discover what lay within the room, Raghavan hesitated to enter as he followed Malaimayan, due to the room's daunting appearance. Upon stepping inside, he was immediately overwhelmed by terror. A black panther emerged from the right! Startled, he instinctively shifted slightly to the left. Malaimayan observed this with a knowing expression. Raghavan then noticed it was merely a model. This model was crafted to resemble a lifelike panther, its fierce eyes seemingly fixed on him. The effigy was set in a small wooden frame, sunken into the floor. The frame's dark colour blended into the dim lighting of the room, making it appear as though a black panther was ready to spring on any entrant. Its mouth agape, the panther seemed to glare at Raghavan with menacing fangs.

Raghavan looked around the room. He understood why Malaimayan referred to the animal hall as a marvel. The hall extended the mansion's entire width and reached inward for forty feet. Construction pillars positioned throughout the hall provided support, and the space was entirely filled with animal and bird models. Malaimayan guided Raghavan through the hall, showing off each of his creations. There were lifelike figures of wild animals like full-sized deer, monkeys, wild cats, bison, and more. A section of the hall featured numerous bird models, including owls. Notably, a Macaw was perched on a wooden frame resembling a tree branch.

Raghavan was drawn in by the sight of the striking parrot and approached it in awe of its design. The parrot, standing one and a half feet tall, had a long tail crafted from genuine, vibrant wings. Its beak and eyes appeared lifelike. After observing the parrot for several minutes, he moved to the hall door. To the left of the entrance, before the black panther model, stood a life-sized sculpted elephant.

Observing the man responsible for numerous wonders standing before him courteously, Raghavan inquired of Malaimayan, "How did you accomplish all this?" Malaimayan replied that "Alan Williams taught everything" and mentioned having invited individuals from overseas to provide training. Raghavan then headed home, considering that Malaimayan was correct about the animal hall being a marvel of the hunting mansion.

Raghavan exited the mansion and addressed Malaimayan, "Grandfather! Please look after your health. If you require any assistance, inform me through someone. I will come immediately." Malaimayan, interrupting Raghavan as he began to depart, gestured for him to pause a moment, and dashed inside the mansion.

After ten minutes, Malaimayan came back holding a box. He handed it to Raghavan, who stood confused at the mansion's gate, wondering why he was being halted. "What is this?" Raghavan asked Malaimayan quizzically. "A present from the old man... for you...! Take it home and see," Malaimayan said with a smile.

As he made his way home after bidding farewell to Malaimayan, the captivating sights from the hunting lodge lingered in his thoughts. The sun gleamed in a clear, azure sky, and the frigid breeze bit into his skin. He relished his walk among the tea plantations in the delightful surroundings. Repeatedly, his mind revisited the animal sculptures he had observed in the hunting lodge. Although he had read about 'Taxidermy' before, he was astonished at how lifelike the animal models appeared. Malaimayan had worked a marvel without any formal training. He recalled how Malaimayan had shown Raghavan a heap of clay and sawdust in the corner of the room and the various materials, ranging from wires to thick iron rods, used to craft the animal models. Raghavan admired him inwardly as an exceptional artist.

As he neared the house, thoughts filled his mind. He suddenly noticed the box he was holding. What could Malaimayan's present be inside that seemingly weightless box? Intrigued, he entered the house, sat in the front room, and began to open the box.

Soon, he realized what was inside. Malaimayan had given him the Macaw parrot specimen in a cardboard box, which he had been observing with interest in the animal hall. After taking it out and appreciating it once more, he searched for a spot to place it. He cleared some books from the table set up for Poonkuzhali in the front room next to the bedroom and positioned the Macaw in the centre of the table. He believed the room itself had become more attractive.

It had been three months since Raghavan visited the hunting lodge and encountered Malaimayan. Poonkuzhali's annual examinations were nearing, and they would conclude in a month's time. He was mindful of the need to discuss her continued education with Uthamaraj and Teacher Radhika. Meeting Teacher Radhika first was essential. It might be difficult to see her post-exams due to the holiday break. Therefore, he resolved to visit the school the following day to meet Teacher Radhika.

He considered departing from home at eleven in the morning, as that was his usual time to meet her during the lunch break. He recalled that he was going to see Radhika after several months. It might not be feasible to meet her again. He thought about giving a gift to Radhika. She had been very helpful and done many Favors for Poonkuzhali. As he scanned the house, nothing stood out to him. Then his gaze fell upon the Macaw on the table. He decided to give it away.

He placed the parrot inside the same cardboard box that Malaimayan had provided. He then put the box in a plastic bag and departed. Raghavan paused at Manikandan's shop and mentioned he was heading to the school to see Poonkuzhali before hurrying down the road. Manikandan was aware that whenever Raghavan visited Poonkuzhali, he also sees Radhika teacher. Although unaware of Raghavan's agenda that day, Manikandan had a notion in mind, and if things unfolded as he imagined, he would be pleased.

Raghavan arrived at school at noon, and he was permitted entry since there weren't any classes in session. When he appeared before Radhika, her face beamed with joy. The unexpected meeting amazed her after a considerable time. She guided him to the hostel, mentioning that 'Poonkuzhali is preparing for the exam in the hostel.'

When he arrived at her room in the hostel, Raghavan announced, "Teacher! I've come to speak with you." Radhika was taken aback. "Alright, please sit," she replied as she took a seat and focused on him. Raghavan briefly discussed how 'Radhika teacher had assisted Poonkuzhali thus far and she is almost finished with her schooling. She should pursue higher education.' He asked Radhika for her advice and suggestions regarding Poonkuzhali's college education. Raghavan's request pleasantly surprised Radhika, as she had already been contemplating Poonkuzhali's further education, and she began sharing her thoughts with Raghavan.

"A bright child, such as Poonkhuzali, ought to be encouraged to pick a reputable college for her education. Attending one located in the capital city is preferable. This is because, in addition to her academic abilities, Poonkuzhali possesses other inherent skills. It is crucial to guide and equip her for the civil services examination, as she is truly deserving of this opportunity," she stated with conviction, and added, "I am willing to assist if she requires any support in this matter."

It felt as though a path had been unlocked in Raghavan's mind. He gazed at Radhika with gratitude and remarked, "Poonkuzhali is fortunate to have a teacher like you." Radhika responded, "I feel lucky as well to have met people like you." Once their discussion concluded, he stood up, mentioning he would consult a friend and inform her of the result. Radhika followed his lead and stood up. Raghavan handed her the gift bag he had brought. As she accepted it and looked inside, she started to say, "what...?" Raghavan explained, "This is my present on Poonkuzhali's behalf. Please open it after I leave," and he departed the room without waiting for her response.

Just as he was about to step out, Radhika quickly followed him and halted him, saying "Hold on a moment," then quickly returned to her room and emerged right away. She carried a small cardboard box with her. Handing it to Raghavan, she said, "This is a present for your wife. Take it home to her." Raghavan stumbled back, speechless, unsure of how to respond. Radhika observed him leave with a smile, amused by his reaction.

After Raghavan vanished from her view, she rushed into the room and fetched the box he had presented her with. Curious about what might be inside the grimy box, she dismantled the contents and stood up. A Macaw parrot, standing one and a half feet tall, perched on her hands, staring at her. Immersed in joy, it was as if she had forgotten the rest of the world. She felt an elation akin to flying. The lifelike appearance of the toy captivated her. She gently placed it on the table and lovingly tapped it with her hands. She was filled with overwhelming joy and amazement when she understood that its wings resembled those of a real parrot. She tenderly stroked the parrot's back and head repeatedly, suddenly imparting a kiss on the parrot in a gesture of gratitude!

Raghavan's home environment was unusual. Upon arriving, he placed the box on the table and proceeded with his afternoon tasks. He was hesitant to open the box. Radhika's teacher had said, "Take it to your wife and present it," leaving him to wonder if there was any other interpretation. He lacked the bravery to open the box then. However, by evening, he managed to calm himself and got ready to open the gift box.

The small box was encased in a lovely, glowing wrapping and bore the inscription "Love Saru! Radhika...!" It was inscribed. With a touch of reluctance, he opened the top layer of paper and took off the lid of the box from within, then sat down, shocked. Inside he found a tiny amount of cereal mix, just like what Poonkuzhali would bring to Saru from Manikandan's store. Raghavan realized that Radhika was revealing the truth of his pretense with this modest gift. He concluded that the only course of action was to apologize for his conduct. An unseen barrier emerged between them.

The following morning, he had an urgent task. He needed to see Uthamaraj right away. Even though he hadn't been visiting Manikandan's shop recently, he went there to inquire about Uthamaraj. Manikandan informed him that Uthamaraj had been relocated to another forest region and would not return to the Athimedu area for at least three years. Although Raghavan felt disappointed, Manikandan reassured him by saying, "Raghava...! You can find him at his office" and provided the office address. Fortunately, Raghavan encountered him at the office.

Uthamaraj reassured Raghavan and happily consented to assist with Poonkuzhali's higher studies upon learning all about her. He said, "Have Poonkuzhali visit me once more after she finishes her exams." By that time, he vowed to reach out to a friend of his in the capital to set up some arrangements.

Time passed swiftly with Raghavan's thoughts. Poonkuzhali had finished her exams and completed her schooling successfully. Raghavan contacted Poonkuzhali and had another meeting with Uthamaraj, which also went as well as he anticipated.

Uthamaraj fulfilled his promise by making the necessary arrangements. He planned to take Poonkuzhali with him to meet his friend 'Narendiran' in the capital. He mentioned that 'his friend is an IAS officer who chooses deserving underprivileged students and assists them in pursuing higher education.' He added that "if Poonkuzhali is fortunate, she will receive his support." Uthamaraj stated that 'he intends to travel to the capital in two days and has arranged for Poonkuzhali to meet his friend.' Raghavan and Poonkuzhali returned with immense happiness. Poonkuzhali was eager about the trip to the capital and meeting new people, her conversation brimming with enthusiasm.

That morning was when Poonkuzhali was meant to leave for the capital with Uthamaraj. She stood before Manikandan's shop, carrying enough provisions for two days while Chitra and Raghavan waited beside her. As they had anticipated, Uthamaraj arrived. Poonkuzhali joyfully got into the vehicle, carrying her belongings in the bag Raghavan had provided. Manikandan emerged from the shop, and the three of them, standing below, waved their hands. Chitra looked cheerful, but Manikandan's expression revealed a slightly dull mind. Raghavan reassured him and led him away.

The trio endured two days of suffering. On the third day in the afternoon, Poonkuzhali arrived at Athimedu alongside Uthamaraj. Uthamaraj brought positive news for all. "Poonkuzhali was victorious. She was fortunate!" he announced loudly as he exited the vehicle. By then, Poonkuzhali hurried over and joyfully clasped Raghavan's hand.

Uthamaraj recounted the happenings to the trio. His friend evaluated Poonkuzhali through several tests and was impressed by her abilities, agreeing to admit her into his training program. He personally arranged for her to continue her education at a nearby women's college. Uthamaraj mentioned that Poonkuzhali would need to depart in a week. He stated he would accompany Poonkuzhali himself and allow Raghavan to join him, after which he departed.

A week later, they found themselves waiting once more at the same location. This time, as Poonkuzhali and Raghavan prepared to board the vehicle, Uthamaraj reassured Manikandan, who appeared bewildered: "There's no need to worry; you're leaving your child in capable hands. Just wait and see." With determination and trust, Poonkuzhali embarked on her journey to the city.

Chapter 21

Newcomer

Poonkuzhali travelled to the capital to pursue an undergraduate degree in Social Science, and she was preparing for her final year exams. Additionally, updates from Uthamaraj indicated that she was excelling in her Indian civil service exam training. Raghavan, Manikandan, and Chitra were very proud of Poonkuzhali's achievements. Raghavan felt that the day when his hopes for Poonkuzhali would come true was approaching soon.

Inside the hunting mansion, Malaimayan was involved in a clandestine activity. Upon exiting the mansion, he displayed a profound sense of relief, having successfully accomplished a significant task. He was confident that it would remain undiscovered. However, elsewhere, a threat was emerging for the item that Malaimayan had kept secure for over ten years. This threat was quickly approaching him.

That afternoon, as Malaimayan was confident that the material was secure with him, a man was released from a central prison. He was about thirty-five years old, strong, and had been serving a life sentence. He couldn't even recall how many years he'd spent inside. He had an urgent task to complete, something he had left unfinished. Immediately upon his release, he began to reflect on it. He had a substantial amount of cash with him, money earned from his prison work. If he chose to hold onto that money and find some employment, he might enjoy a peaceful life. However, his restless mind had other plans, driven by anger. What dangers might arise from the rash decisions of this defiant man!

Just ten minutes after he got to the jail entrance, he started behaving true to his nature. He quickly crossed the bustling street ahead and headed to the small shop nearby. There, he purchased a cigarette and smoked it, lost in thought about his future actions.

Following his plan, he initially visited a salon to alter his appearance. Upon leaving, he no longer had a beard and Mustache and had shortened his hair. Subsequently, he purchased brown-tinted eyewear with thin frames and donned it, along with adding a cap to his ensemble, to finalize his transformation. His objective was to ensure no one in his hometown would identify him.

He purchased just enough clothes to meet his basic needs and took an autorickshaw to the bus station. Without any further consideration, he set off for his hometown. On the first day, he arrived at the base of the hill and stayed there overnight. The following day, he travelled by bus towards the hill into his hometown. As he ascended, memories of past events from years ago filled his thoughts.

The item he nearly held slipped from view but remained vivid in his memory. 'Who was that person? Where did he originate from? The object that fell, rolled, and settled right in front of him. He picked it up and placed it in his pocket. However, it was missing afterwards...! Who was the old, skeletal man who appeared out of nowhere? Perhaps the old man took it?' These questions incessantly plagued his mind, yet answers eluded him. He had even prepared to sell the item once he obtained it. He realized things had proceeded too quickly that day. He resolved not to act so impulsively in the future.

The bus arrived in the hill town and was heading to the bus station. He snapped out of his reflections and glanced outside. The site where the old carpenter had been strangled a decade ago in the toddy shop came into view. Che...! Regretting the decision to kill the old man. Rash decisions... all was lost. Due to numerous witnesses at the scene in the toddy shop, his conviction was swift. Even after serving a lengthy sentence, he remained unchanged. He intended to pick up the game right where he had paused. Destiny...!

The day following his arrival in the mountainous town, he began his search. His starting point was the hunting mansion. He departed early that morning, heading to Athimedu, and then walked towards the mansion. As he neared the hunting mansion, the profound silence of the area enveloped him. He approached the mansion from the south, heading to the entrance, a place he knew well. The front door stood open. He reached the doorstep and quietly gazed inside.

The Amman statue appeared to gaze at him from the first floor. He shifted his focus to the goddess's crown. The area where the crown's stone once was appeared unrefined. The absence of the stone there clearly suggested it had been taken by someone.

He remained on the portico instead of entering the mansion, where he fell and dropped the sharp weapon he was holding. Without his knowledge, feet emerged from the portico and began clearing the thick growth and disturbing the soil. He discovered the tool he had been searching for. He moved and retrieved what had been buried in the earth. He used his hands to brush off the soil that had accumulated on it. It was a 'screwdriver,' long buried beneath the ground, with the handle intact but the rest completely rusted. As he pressed the blunt end with the fingers of his left hand and turned around, he was startled. Malaimayan stood before him on the portico, looking menacing with his eyes blazing red with anger.

The newcomer had been anticipating opportunities like this, so he quickly composed himself and recognized that the elderly man before him was the one he had kicked, causing him to fall years ago. At that point, Malaimayan demanded angrily, "Who are you...! What is your job here?" The newcomer remained lost in thought, ignoring the elder's queries. He thought to himself, 'The old man is still around,' and considered, "Can I kill him right now and find the diamond!" He tightened his grip on the handle of the tool he held firmly. A moment later, he decided otherwise and stated, "I have started a new position here in the tea estate. I'm here to see if I can find a place to live," he told Malaimayan with a composed expression.

Malaimayan was skeptical of his words. To minimize conversation and get him to leave, he instructed, "Stay away! Head over there and inquire." He gestured toward the Athimedu residential area. Realizing that further interaction with the old man would be unwise, he tersely replied, "Alright," tossed the tool he was holding back into the plants, glanced at Malaimayan, and proceeded to walk where Malaimayan had gestured.

Malaimayan observed the new man as he walked. Malaimayan harboured unpleasant feelings about the stranger. He found the man's walk somewhat recognizable but couldn't fully recall it. His amnesia was worsening, causing old memories to fade from his mind.

Raghavan felt very excited when he woke up in the morning. The reason for his excitement was the news he received from Uthamaraj on the previous day. He had visited the office on the first day to inquire about Poonkuzhali. Poonkuzhali had finished her final year exams and was dedicating her time to practicing for the civil services exam. She needed to take the preliminary exam within a month. If her results, due in two weeks, were favourable, she would have to prepare for the main and final exams over the next two months. This information fuelled Raghavan's enthusiasm. He got ready to visit Manikandan's shop to share this news with him.

He exited the house and observed the paved road ahead. The two-wheeler traffic was heavier than usual. There were also people gathered at Manikandan's shop. The sky was overcast, with clouds drifting northeast, showing no sign of rain. He made his way to the shop and sat down on the wooden bench. Even then, he noticed two-wheelers frequently traveling along the road towards the dam and onward to the city. Traffic has grown over the past decade, which has also brought more customers to Manikandan's shop. Raghavan couldn't even remember why he had come. Customers continued to arrive.

He waited until the shop was empty of customers and completed his conversation with Manikandan. Meanwhile, a long vehicle arrived on the road and parked in front of the shop. The driver and a few companions exited the vehicle and entered the shop. Raghavan noticed the vehicle and discovered it contained parts for constructing an iron tower. While Manikandan was occupied making tea for the visitors, he considered asking them about the vehicle's contents. At that moment, a Jeep arrived and parked behind the larger vehicle, and Uthamaraj stepped out.

Raghavan was taken aback to encounter him. He realized that despite their meeting at the office the day before, nothing was mentioned. Soon, he approached and took a seat next to Raghavan. He was equally pleased to see Raghavan at the shop. He began speaking without any prompting from Raghavan.

"The vehicle has brought the necessary components to establish a cell phone tower," he mentioned, pointing to the vehicle. "A location has been chosen for it on a ridge, not far from Kondarapatti. You'll notice many vehicles coming this way from now on." He pulled a mobile phone device from his pocket and showed it to Raghavan. "Once the tower is up, you'll be able to reach others with this kind of phone." Raghavan had seen such a compact mobile device but had never used one. Additionally, Uthamaraj informed Raghavan that the dam region was now under his oversight and that he would also patrol the Athimedu area. Since the tower's designated site was within the forest, he was appointed as a special superintendent to safeguard both animals and humans from harm. At that moment, the group in the large vehicle was prepared to resume their journey. Uthamaraj accompanied them to Kondarapatti, leaving the shop deserted.

Within a few minutes, the stranger appeared from behind the shop and approached. To Raghavan, he looked somewhat peculiar. With just a month until the rains were to begin, the weather was neither sunny nor snowy. Nonetheless, the unfamiliar man wore a snug headdress over his ears and sported glasses to shield his eyes. He wasn't someone Raghavan had seen in the vicinity before. As Raghavan was pondering over inquiring from Manikandan, the stranger asked Manikandan for a filter-cigarette.

Manikandan took a cigarette from the pack and offered it to him. The newcomer declined and instead purchased a full pack and a matchbox. He then moved to the side of the shop and vanished. Moments later, the sound of a match being struck and a continuous stream of cigarette smoke came from the side of the shop. With a gesture, Raghavan asked Manikandan, "Who is that?" Manikandan shrugged as if he didn't know. "Seems to be a stranger," he said quietly, bowing slightly, his voice only audible to Raghavan.

Meanwhile, another event caught Raghavan's attention. A group of parrots flew noisily across the sky over the store. This immediately reminded him of Saru, and he thought that perhaps Saru had arrived, which prompted him to leave. He informed Manikandan and promptly made his way back home. The man smoking next to the shop noticed Raghavan limping with the help of his crutch. He observed until Raghavan entered his house. Disposing of his cigarette on the ground, he proceeded towards the tea plant.

At home, Raghavan was lost in contemplation. Resting in his palm was a small piece of clay, given to him by Saru. The incident puzzled him greatly. He had noticed flocks of parrots soaring through the valley and sometimes witnessed them returning in significant numbers from the direction of the hunting mansion. Saru always accompanied these flocks, but where did they originate? Discovering that could unravel the mystery of the clay. While it seemed insignificant, his intuition said otherwise. He somehow felt compelled to find the answer. Suddenly, it occurred to him that Malaimayan might possess some insights on this matter, as parrots also flew from the direction of the mansion. He resolved to consult Malaimayan.

Chapter 22

Clay Pieces

Determined to uncover the truth about the lump of clay, Raghavan carried the tin box filled with his clay collection and set off to the hunting mansion to meet Malaimayan.

After returning from the shop, Raghavan soon made his way to the hunting mansion carrying the tin box containing the clay lumps. The man who had left the shop before Raghavan was now perched on the stone stage, absorbed in smoking a cigarette and deep in thought. This man noticed a lame figure, whom he had seen at the shop, approaching through the tea garden. Prompted by some instinct, he quickly extinguished his cigarette by crushing it with his foot, then rushed to conceal himself behind the peepal tree.

While pondering over the details he needed to inquire about and learn from Malaimayan, Raghavan abruptly halted as he crossed the stone stage. A few discarded cigarette butts lying nearby drew his attention. The image of the unfamiliar man he noticed at Manikandan's shop popped into his mind. He realized that this individual might have been seated at the stone stage, smoking. Without further contemplation, he resumed his walk.

When Raghavan made his way over the stone stage, the newcomer emerged from behind the peepal tree. He observed Raghavan as he moved through the tea plants. Though uncertain of the reason, he felt a thrill that his caution had been rewarded so quickly. At that moment, Raghavan veered off the path in the direction of the hunting mansion. The newcomer swiftly entered the tea garden, crouched among the tea plants, concealed himself, and began trailing Raghavan.

Raghavan stepped into the hunting mansion's grounds, where trees and plants from the tea garden surrounded him in silence. He gradually approached Malaimayan's residence, which was attached to the hunting mansion on the north side. It was a tiny house, and the door stood open. Inside, it was somewhat dim due to insufficient lighting.

As Raghavan stepped into the compact outhouse, he found Malaimayan busy preparing a meal in the kitchen. Raghavan was taken aback that Malaimayan was managing by himself despite his age. Equally, Malaimayan was startled to find Raghavan standing at the entrance. He stood up and welcomed Raghavan inside. With no chair available, Raghavan promptly seated himself on the floor. Malaimayan joined him on the ground, observing Raghavan as if wondering what the issue was.

At that point, the newcomer who had trailed Raghavan concealed himself behind a tree close to the hunting mansion and began observing Malaimayan's house intently.

With the intention of explaining to Malaimayan the purpose of his visit, Raghavan unlatched the box he was holding and revealed the clay lumps within to Malaimayan.

Taking the box without comprehending, Malaimayan inspected what was inside. He then picked up a piece, crushed it between his fingers, broke it apart, and sniffed it. "Where did you obtain this from?" he inquired. Raghavan then briefly mentioned Saru and explained that it was the parrot who had brought these clay pieces.

Malaimayan got the message, though the parrot's behaviour caught him off guard. Observing the expression on Malaimayan's face, Raghavan realized that he was already aware of the situation. "Do you know, grandpa?" he asked, curious. Malaimayan motioned for him to be patient, stood up, and gazed out over the valley through the window. "It will arrive shortly," he remarked. Unclear about what Malaimayan was alluding to, Raghavan refrained from questioning him further. Without uttering a word, Malaimayan crouched under the stove, stoked the fire with more wood to intensify it, checked the rice by stirring it with a spoon after removing the pot's lid, then replaced the lid and diminished the fire by taking out the wood. Returning to the window, he spent a few moments examining the valley before saying to Raghavan, "Alright, let's move..."

Raghavan rose without a word and trailed Malaimayan. Outside the hunting mansion, Malaimayan pushed aside the foliage and proceeded toward a distant mud slope. Raghavan continued along the same path. After a few minutes of effort, they paused in the underbrush approximately twenty feet from the slope in front of them. Malaimayan gestured for Raghavan to remain silent as he waited. Opposite them, Raghavan observed the slope a fifty-foot-wide expanse of bare earth, devoid of any plants, even vines. Standing silently with

Malaimayan, Raghavan was puzzled as to whom they were waiting for.

Observing Malaimayan and the cripple departing from the house and distancing themselves from the shrubs in front of the mansion, the newcomer approached Malaimayan's house, traversed the mansion's portico, and proceeded to the opposite side of the thickly wooded area to observe them.

Malaimayan, positioned within the shelter of the bushes and anticipating something, prepared himself. He nudged Raghavan and directed him to gaze at the sky. While Raghavan didn't see anything right away, he began to hear birds from afar, and shortly after, countless parrots started to swirl in the air above him. They filled the area with their 'kee...kee...kee... kee...' calls. Before long, all the parrots flying above descended towards the mudslide ahead and perched on it as if clinging. Some parrots were perched on the vines and trees near the mudslide and would then fly to the mudslide or from it to nearby trees, all while emitting continuous screeches.

Raghavan was captivated by the incredible sight he had never witnessed before. Thousands of parrots were right before his eyes...! He was thrilled. Malaimayan touched Raghavan again and encouraged him to watch the parrots perched on the mudslide. He was astonished to see some of them ingesting the bits of soil they had seized. Numerous parrots took a piece of soil, flew to nearby trees, perched, and consumed it. The spectacle he observed was astonishing to him. He had never even known that parrots consumed clay.

The person concealed behind the tree was equally astonished to witness thousands of parrots simultaneously. He observed them by shifting to a couple of different trees among the chattering parrots and crouching behind the shrubs.

Raghavan felt as though he could have observed the parrots indefinitely. However, Malaimayan disrupted the calm by aggressively shaking the bush before him, creating a sudden disturbance. In an instant, all the parrots perched on the mud slope, nearby trees, branches, and vines, cheering, took off together into the sky. As Raghavan trailed their movement, the flock of birds flew off into the distance and vanished.

Silence once more descended on the area, making the preceding events seem like a mystical vision. Malaimayan grasped Raghavan's hand and led him away from the shrubs toward the muddy slope. The clay mound was damp from occasional rainfall. Malaimayan touched the landslide with his hands, demonstrated it to Raghavan, and removed a small piece of clay. He crushed it between his fingers and sniffed it, then brought it near Raghavan's nose. Raghavan also picked a bit from the clay mound with his fingers. It was apparent that the soil pieces Saru had brought were sourced from there.

The newcomer, having watched a lot in the bush, couldn't grasp what was occurring. The parrots perched on the mud-slope, flew, and chirped, while the old, disabled man approached the mound and used his fingers to pick at it, leaving him bewildered.

Malaimayan grasped Raghavan's hand and began retracing his steps. While walking, he mentioned that he had watched the spectacle numerous times since relocating to the hunting lodge. It was Alan Williams who introduced it to him. He added that Alan Williams took great pleasure in the event. Additionally, Alan Williams provided some insights into why parrots consume bits of clay.

Malaimayan went on to explain, "Parrots consume a range of fruits, nuts, and seeds, some of which could be toxic. They ingest clay to neutralize the toxins. Additionally, certain nutrients in the clay are absorbed into their bodies." By then, they had returned to Malaimayan's home.

As they both headed to the mansion's side, the newcomer rose and left the bushes, approaching the mound of clay. He used his hands to scrape the slope of soil. The adhesive wet clay clung to his hands. Uncomfortably, he sensed its texture, spread his palms, and walked toward the trees where he had been hiding earlier.

At Malaimayan's residence, Raghavan noticed Saru's actions. It had been bringing him pieces of clay from this place as a continued gesture of gratitude for saving it in the past. Indeed, it was offering him the clay fragments as food. For a moment, he considered whether he could consume the piece of clay in front of Saru.

Raghavan's reason for visiting Malaimayan's house was fulfilled, and he was ready to depart. However, before he could leave, Raghavan felt uneasy about informing Malaimayan of his frail condition. Misinterpreting Raghavan's hesitance, Malaimayan assured him, "Brother, it is secure with me. I will disclose it at the right moment." Raghavan glanced at Malaimayan, considering saying, 'I don't want to hear that actually,' but he reconsidered, quietly turning back to the door. It appeared it might begin to rain soon.

Pleased that Raghavan had discovered the truth about the lumps of clay, he departed from Malaimayan's residence, walked into the tea garden, and began heading towards his home. Meanwhile, behind the mansion in the other direction, the man observed him, wiping the mud off his hands on the trees.

Simultaneously, a light drizzle began and, without warning, turned into a heavy downpour within seconds. In just a few minutes, Raghavan was soaked through. He had neither the time nor the way to avoid the rain, so Raghavan walked home while getting drenched.

The newcomer on the opposite side of the mansion experienced the same situation. He too was soaked by the rain and proceeded to the tea plant before departing the area.

Raghavan arrived back home soaked from the rain. It was only upon arriving home that he recalled he had forgotten the tin box with the clay pieces at Malaimayan's place. The rain was pouring heavily. He didn't feel the need for the box immediately. He planned that the following day or when it stopped raining, he could go and retrieve it.

The actions of the newcomer in the morning at the hunting lodge had disturbed Malaimayan to some extent. At that moment, he realized the clay pieces box was present. He picked up the box and went inside the lodge. In the animal hall, he set it down beside the clay heap in the left corner and then went back.

In the city, the thief's thoughts were in a whirl. The morning's events at the hunting mansion kept replaying in his mind. Why did the old man visit the clay mound with the crippled man? What did he reveal to him there? It remained unclear. By that time, the old man seemed so fragile in his mind that a couple of slaps could topple him. The lame man was also not powerful. He figured that should he get involved, he might be able to handle them both.

He believed the stone was likely hidden in that mansion. The moment it crossed his mind, he recalled it slipping from his grasp and grew furious. 'Once the old man is pressured, he'll reveal the truth. Grab it, sell it at the shop, and then quickly escape from here.' These considerations turned into concrete plans. He had coordinated his scheme with a jeweller in the hill town.

All he needed was to pick an appropriate day to carry out his plan. He believed that evening would be the ideal time on a day with nonstop rain. Continuous rain would mean no one would be out and about, and the darkness of evening would aid him. With his plan fixed, he waited for the anticipated day, which came sooner than expected. However, what he anticipated was different from what transpired!

Chapter 23

Malaimayan's Demise

The rainy season had started in Athimedu, and it was raining every day. Raghavan was held up at home unable to go anywhere outside. Uthamaraj did not come to the Manikandan's shop. So, there was no information about Poonkuzhali. From time to time, the thought of getting back the tin box containing the pieces of clay that had been forgotten in the Malaimayan house, kept appearing in his mind. Saru's compassion and affection was contained in it. A few hours without rain would be enough to bring it back. But the rain kept getting heavier and heavier.

The circumstances proved advantageous for the thief. As he anticipated, the rain began to pour without stopping. That day, it had been pouring heavily since morning, and the sky was laden with rain clouds, making daytime seem like night. He concluded that this day was the most opportune for him.

He departed before dusk. Amidst the pouring rain, clad in a raincoat that shielded him from head to toe, he rushed towards the hunting mansion for the hunt. With no weapon in hand, there was no requirement for that elderly man. As he stepped into the tea plantations surrounding the hunting mansion, he glanced around. Other than him, the area was deserted, and the valley remained silent.

He made his way through the tea garden to the hunting lodge under the rain. Despite his raincoat, he was soaked to the skin. As he travelled, water flowed down the hillside in small streams heading toward the lake. With a firm resolve, he arrived at the hunting mansion.

With confidence and without stealth, he stood at the entrance of the mansion and peered inside. The statue of the goddess on the opposite side was the first thing that drew his attention. The crown on the goddess's head provoked his anger. The stone from it had fallen and rolled to just where he was standing, rekindling his fury. He recalled the old man's deceit in taking the stone that day. The memory intensified his anger toward Malaimayan, and with that same anger, he descended onto the portico and swiftly made his way to Malaimayan's house. Upon reaching the house, he found Malaimayan in the cooking area. In the dim light inside, Malaimayan's presence was not apparent. He moved down from the doorway and paused two steps inside.

Malaimayan approached in disbelief when he unexpectedly noticed someone inside the house soaked from the rain. Observing the frail old man standing before, the furious individual became enraged. With the same intensity, he struck Malaimayan hard in the chest. The force of the kick hurled Malaimayan into the kitchen, where he landed among the dishes. No cries were heard from Malaimayan, only the clattering of dishes. The assailant swiftly followed, dragging him by his legs into the front room. Without pausing, he pressed his boot against Malaimayan's neck and leaned forward to gaze at his face.

Malaimayan was clueless about the events unfolding around him. Who was attacking him? And for what reason? He was completely bewildered. The strike to his chest brought intense agony throughout his body. He had no energy left to cry out, nor could he speak as a foot pressed heavily on his neck. Like squashing a bug, the attacker yelled, "Where is the red stone?" The shout cut through the noise of the rain, making Malaimayan grasp the situation. Shaking and clutching the leg that pinned him down, Malaimayan pleaded silently with his eyes, overwhelmed by the torment.

Believing the elderly man was approaching to speak, the thief removed the foot pressing on his neck and said, "Alright, speak now." Even in his deathly agony, Malaimayan attempted to protect the diamond. In a weak voice, he murmured "don't know." Upon hearing this, the thief was enraged and struck Malaimayan's left leg with the same foot that had crushed the old man. A soft 'kadak...' was heard as Malaimayan's leg became limp. The bone beneath the knee was fractured in two, rendering the leg useless. Malaimayan's entire body trembled. The chest heaved intensely with each breath. Both hands desperately searched for something to hold onto. The mouth was twisted.

Malaimayan's cries of agony blended with the rain's sound and faded away. He was out cold. The thief, deciding the location was unsuitable for further questioning, began pulling Malaimayan towards the mansion. As they reached the portico, Malaimayan began to moan softly. Hearing this, the thief set him down on the portico and attentively listened to the sounds escaping his lips.

As Malaimayan regained awareness, he raised his left hand and muttered something. The word 'clay' was the only part that was heard distinctly by the attentive listener. Malaimayan then lost consciousness once more. Hearing the word 'clay' triggered numerous thoughts in the thief's mind. Earlier, the old man had taken the disabled man to a clay slope, showing him something. A new thought struck him. Despite the rain, he was confident that if he led the old man to the clay mound, he would reveal something significant. Determined to act at once, he seized Malaimayan's hands and pulled him through the thorny thicket.

He found it effortless to haul Malaimayan's body, which resembled a bag of bones. Upon reaching the clay mound and shifting Malaimayan to the left, his broken left leg got trapped in a nearby bush. He gave a strong pull to release the leg tangled in the bush. Suddenly, the leg dislodged, and simultaneously, a silver bead from the anklet popped off, landing and embedding itself in the clay mound nearby. After dragging the liberated body back, he placed it where he had been before with the lame and leaned down to observe Malaimayan. Malaimayan remained still, his eyes wide open, as if gazing at raindrops descending from the sky. The raindrops landed on his eyes and flowed down.

Malaimayan lost half of his vitality when the thief aggressively fractured his leg. As he was pulled through the wet foliage, whatever life he had left slipped away. It took the thief a few moments to grasp that Malaimayan was lifeless. Realizing his impulsive actions once more, he sat beside the corpse, unsure of his next move. The rain continued to soak them, with nightfall fast approaching.

He noticed the light fading around him and quickly rose to act according to his thoughts. He retrieved Malaimayan's body, took it to Malaimayan's house, and placed it before the doorway, positioning the arms in front of the head to suggest a fall upon exiting the house. He then proceeded to investigate the trail where he had dragged Malaimayan, but the rain had erased the drag marks.

He needed to find what he was looking for. Darkness was starting to gather. He hurriedly dashed into the mansion. With the same urgency, he began searching every corner of the mansion. The reception room downstairs and the rooms on either side of the animal hall were devoid of any objects. He swiftly went upstairs and entered the room where Alan Williams had been staying. That was also empty, giving him no room to explore. He thumped back down and ran into the animal hall. It was there he realized how misguided his choices had been.

The Animal Hall was shrouded in darkness. He struggled in vain to see anything within the space. Despite his cautious attempts, he collided with several animal specimens and ended up tumbling to the ground with them. Frustrated and displeased, he exited the mansion and returned to Malaimayan's residence.

He carefully stepped over Malaimayan's body, which lay by the entrance, and went inside. He examined and overturned every item he could find, searching frantically. The item he sought was elusive. Eventually, he found a straw box amidst a heap of clothes in a corner and opened it. Inside was a silver anklet, which he took and examined in the room's faint light. He slipped it into his pocket, realizing there were no other places left to search. As he headed back out, the chain on Malaimayan's left leg caught his attention. It was the matching anklet to the one he had just found. He quickly detached it from Malaimayan's leg, pocketed it, and rose to his feet. The darkness was all-encompassing, and the rain continued unabated. Disheartened, he saw no reason to remain any longer and departed from the hunting mansion's vicinity.

In the early morning, it felt a bit more peaceful once the rain ceased. The sky was sufficiently clear, suggesting that the clouds had all transformed into rain. That day, the sun, absent for several days, appeared rapidly, and cast its rays, illuminating and warming the valley region.

Raghavan felt at ease when the morning rain subsided. The clear sky seen through the window and the bright sun outside offered reassurance that the rain wouldn't return that day. He pondered the idea of visiting Malaimayan's house to retrieve his box of clay pieces. Quickly preparing himself, he completed his morning tasks swiftly and departed for Malaimayan's house.

Raghavan strolled by Manikandan's dwelling and stepped into the tea garden. Having been confined at home by the continuous rain for several days, Raghavan found the warmth of the morning to be particularly delightful. He merrily traversed the tea garden and descended into the stone stage area. In the distance, he noticed an unusual scene near the hunting mansion. Normally deserted, the sudden appearance of people in the area startled him. He observed both men and women moving towards the hunting mansion. Quickening his pace, he crossed the stone stage zone and reached the adjacent tea plantations, where a wave of anxiety swept over him. From that vantage point, he could clearly see the hunting mansion alongside Malaimayan's house. Approximately ten or fifteen individuals had gathered at Malaimayan's doorstep, closely observing something on the ground. The sight of women there, partially veiling their faces with sarees, alerted Raghavan to some misfortune that might have occurred there.

Raghavan hastened his steps. As he neared the Malaimayan residence, anxiety crept in, causing a slight tremble in his body. The crowd noticed Raghavan and stepped aside to allow him through. Once the crowd cleared, the sight before him hit him like a slap. His recent suspicions were confirmed. Malaimayan was lying there lifeless. Those beside him remarked, "Perhaps he came out of the house, fell, and passed away. How much more can someone over a hundred years old endure?" They spoke as if they had seen Malaimayan's death with their own eyes. Raghavan shared the same thought as he looked at Malaimayan's body.

The officers who arrived promptly shared the same viewpoint. Aside from a fractured leg, Malaimayan showed no other injuries. The police swiftly determined that his death resulted from an accident. They began organizing the removal of the body for formal investigations. A significant crowd assembled near the hunting mansion upon noticing the series of police vehicles and the accompanying ambulance.

The authorities completed their investigation and placed Malaimayan's body onto a stretcher before sealing off his residence and hunting lodge. Raghavan eventually ceased watching Malaimayan's body. A few minutes later, Malaimayan's body was carried past him on the stretcher, with his fractured left leg moving across his view as it swayed with the movement.

After several minutes, the crowd surrounding him thinned out, leaving Raghavan standing alone at Malaimayan's doorstep, filled with deep sorrow. Suddenly, a thought flickered in his mind, clear enough for him to grasp. It was about Malaimayan's fractured left leg. There was something absent from that leg, something that kept surfacing in his thoughts. Within moments, he recalled what it was the silver anklet that Malaimayan always wore on his left leg was not there. He glanced toward the direction where the stretcher had been taken. Malaimayan's body had been placed into the ambulance, which was now departing. Subsequently, the crowd that had gathered began to scatter.

Raghavan discovered some truths through the absence of Malaimayan's anklet. It dawned on him that Malaimayan's demise was no accident. 'This could be the second casualty linked to the red diamond, a decade after the first. Once more, the same killer has surfaced.' He deduced that the culprit stole the diamond from Malaimayan and murdered him. But what could he do about it? No solutions came to him. He lingered there for some time and then quietly went back home.

The killer stood amidst the scattering crowd, observing Raghavan with perplexity. Noticing Raghavan lingering outside Malaimayan's house for an extended period, he pondered, 'What connection might the old man have with the cripple?' Then it dawned on him that he might obtain what he desired by focusing on that feeble individual! Fresh thoughts formed. He resolved to monitor Raghavan. Once Raghavan began his journey home, he, too, departed along with the dispersing throng.

Chapter 24

Silver Anklet Bead

It has been three months since Malaimayan's passing. The rainy season had ended, and the chill was beginning to be noticeable. Raghavan's sorrow over Malaimayan's death had somewhat subsided, but he was having difficulty fully recuperating from its effects. Each time he thought of Malaimayan, the image of his rain-soaked body in the hunting lodge haunted his thoughts. Frequently, it was as if Malaimayan was asking him from some unknown place, 'what was wrong with me?'

Raghavan pondered over what wrongdoing could be attributed to Malaimayan in the events of the past years. Was forming a friendship with Somanathan misplaced? Was it wrong to serve Alan Williams as a reliable employee? Could he be at fault for attempting to safeguard the diamond by sharing its secret with his father Devanathan? What was the reason behind his desire to disclose that secret to Raghavan before dying? Perhaps he thought Raghavan would ensure its protection after his demise. Why let go of the ancestral treasure into the hands of a murderous thief? These persistent questions faded, giving rise to a new one: 'Where exactly is that red diamond?'

Had the thief taken it away, or was it hidden alongside Malaimayan's heart in his grave? If it hadn't been moved, it might still be within the hunting mansion. Malaimayan died before he could reveal the secret to Raghavan. If the thief hadn't captured the diamond, he might persist in his search. This must be prevented. He had already lost his father, and then Malaimayan, who cared for him. More tragedies like these must be avoided. A determination arose within him to locate the diamond and claim it as government property. The most urgent task was uncovering the thief's identity. But how? Where to begin? He found himself without answers, and his mind grew weary.

Simultaneously, an unusual incident connected to the passing of Malaimayan took place near the hunting mansion, specifically in the clay mound across from it.

A massive flock of parrots assembled there to eat clay. Among them was Saru. Saru, like the other birds, flew to the clay mound, perched there, and picked up a small portion of clay. When the clay piece slipped from its beak and dropped, Saru pursued it, swooping down to retrieve it again. Suddenly, for reasons unknown, Saru began rubbing its beak against the ground, trying to dislodge the clay from its mouth. It tilted its head and started to roll over as if it couldn't fly, scraping along the soil, plants, and shrubs.

Its suffering and pain persisted. As the other parrots took flight, it could not join them, flew briefly, and then touched down as if struck, rolling with its beak on the ground. However, it persisted and gradually made its way to Raghavan's house.

Raghavan, feeling drained, sat in the front room lost in thought. Upon hearing a crash at the back door followed by a thud, he went to investigate. There, he found Saru rolling on the floor. Startled, Raghavan sat down and gently cradled Saru in his hands. As Saru settled in his arms, it stopped its agitated movements and began to vocalize at Raghavan, as if seeking solace in him. However, its voice was unclear, struggling as if speaking without a tongue, yet it persisted in expressing its troubles to him in every way possible.

Raghavan took hold of Saru and examined its wings and legs for a few minutes to check if they were injured. Noticing a shift in its cries, he lifted Saru closer to his face to inspect what was wrong with its mouth, but Saru could not open her mouth. He then put it back down, gestured with his hand saying "stay...!", and went inside to bring a thin piece of cloth. Regardless of whether it understood, Saru stayed patiently where he had left her.

Raghavan bound Saru's wings and legs with the fabric he had brought, then carried it to the front room. He gently opened its mouth in the light to examine inside. To his astonishment, a silver bead was lodged on the tip of Saru's tongue. Seated with Saru on his lap, he carefully opened its beak wider and used his fingers to softly dislodge the bead from her tongue, removing it without harming the tongue.

In the following instant, Saru began cheerfully exclaiming 'kee... kee... kee... kee... ok... ok... kee... kee... come... ok... ok... kee... kee... kee... kee...' along with the couple of words it recognized. Raghavan felt great joy, having resolved the issue himself. He quickly uncovered Saru and placed her on the ground. Saru leaped twice and flew up to the curtain rod in his bedroom, as she had done previously. Then, she headed out through the backyard path, calling 'kee... kee... kee... kee...' Once more intrigued, Raghavan trailed it into the backyard. Saru lingered on a fig tree branch, and when he stood beneath it, she called 'kee... kee...' twice. It seemed she was expressing gratitude or something. In the next moment, she spread her wings and took flight, exclaiming 'kee... kee... kee... kee...' Raghavan watched as Saru flew off. Within moments, her cries faded out of his hearing and Saru vanished from his view in the distance.

Raghavan's face reflected sadness as he was unable to accept that Saru had taken off. Stationed under the fig tree, he gazed at the silver bead nestled in his left hand. The wire at the bead's end was somewhat worn and had snapped. It had been forcefully removed from a silver anklet. Yet, how did it end up in Saru's mouth? This question puzzled him.

He entered the house and searched for the box to place the silver bead along with the clay chunks. He recalled that it remained at Malaimayan's place. He stored the silver bead in a different small box. However, the thought of that clay box began to vex him after that. It was distressing for him that it ended up stuck in the hunting lodge.

Three months have passed since Malaimayan's passing, and the mansion remains sealed. The hunting mansion's doors are still locked under a government seal, with no clearance for entry. Raghavan communicated his wish to the tea estate's management, stating that 'there is no heir to care for the mansion after Malaimayan. The mansion, which houses invaluable artefacts crafted by Malaimayan, must be protected not only to save these treasures but also to honour Malaimayan's legacy.' He offered to undertake the maintenance if there were no objections from management. The plantation management agreed and assured him that they would grant permission once the formalities were finalized and an official order to unseal the mansion was issued. Raghavan had to await that moment.

Concurrently, the thief, after taking Malaimayan's life but failing in his mission, set his sights on Raghavan as the next target. He deemed it essential to vigilantly watch Raghavan. On the day of Malaimayan's demise, the unsearched animal hall in the hunting mansion lingered in his thoughts. The individual expected to return and conduct a search the following day, but was met with disappointment, as the mansion had been locked and sealed. He eagerly anticipated the day those doors would reopen. To advance his plan, he secured employment at the tea factory. His time in jail had equipped him with diverse work experience, enabling him to easily secure a position there. Thus, his presence around the tea estate and its surroundings went unnoticed. Meanwhile, he continued to observe the daily happenings around the hunting mansion.

Raghavan regularly spent several hours each morning at Manikandan's store. On that day, while he was sitting there, Uthamaraj arrived. He had some urgent business to attend to, so he briefly stayed, drank tea, and left, assuring them he would return in the evening. The person who had gone to the jeep came back to the shop and told Manikandan and Raghavan that Poonkuzhali had successfully passed the first stage of her exam, completed the final exam, and was now awaiting the results. He mentioned that the results would be announced in three months. Uthamaraj stated that his friend Narendiran, in the capital city, was confident Poonkuzhali would pass the final exam and that she was currently undergoing additional training. With that, he departed. Raghavan and Manikandan exchanged a glance of joy.

Uthamaraj's advice bore fruit in three months, as Poonkuzhali also passed the second exam. Instead of Uthamaraj, it was Poonkuzhali who came to Athimedu to share the news. Manikandan was astonished to see her arrive on the morning bus. She alighted and rushed straight to hug Manikandan. It was then that Manikandan realized something wonderful had occurred. He blessed her by resting his hand on her head and led her to Raghavan. For Raghavan, while he anticipated the news, his happiness was amplified hearing it directly from Poonkuzhali.

Raghavan arrived at her home while Poonkuzhali instructed Manikandan to go to the store. Just as Chitra was departing for work, she unexpectedly felt immense joy upon seeing her daughter standing there. Poonkuzhali knelt and lay prostrate at Chitra's feet. After receiving the news, Chitra kissed her daughter's forehead, led her to the deity's shelf, and applied the kunguma tilak. Poonkuzhali, with the kunguma tilak on her forehead, leaned against the doorstep and tenderly smiled at Raghavan, who was standing outside with his crutch.

Raghavan's mind conjured the image of young Poonkuzhali, who had been leaning on the same step fifteen years back. She stood there in a ragged dress, with a flat head and unkempt hair. Today, she dons stylish attire and has a knowledgeable glow in her smile. A transformation has occurred. She might soon become a collector. The fortune that has aided her thus far seems poised to continue supporting her. His heart brimmed with delight as he reflected on her wisdom. She seized the opportunity adeptly. Raghavan headed home, silently applauding her.

Poonkuzhali got ready and arrived at Raghavan's house in a couple of hours. Finding him absent, she headed directly to the store, sat with Raghavan, and jokingly asked her father for "one cup of tea." Overjoyed, he made tea for the trio and joined them. All of them appreciated the moment and relished it in silence.

Throughout the day, Raghavan and Poonkuzhali spent time in the shop with Manikandan. Poonkuzhali recounted her countryside experiences to them both, and they were delighted to listen. The only downside was her announcement that she needed to return in a week, though she reassured them by explaining her reasons. She expressed with deep emotion her gratitude to Narendiran for his role in training her and aiding her accomplishments. Her eyes showed a hint of distress. Raghavan promptly stood up, respectfully bowed in Narendiran's direction, and then resumed his seat.

After expressing everything, Poonkuzhali requested something from Raghavan. Her request was fair, and he recognized its importance. However, he felt a bit embarrassed and delayed his response. Ignoring his unwillingness, Poonkuzhali made the decision on her own and stated, "Uncle, we'll both visit Radhika teacher tomorrow morning." In response, Raghavan unenthusiastically agreed, saying "OK."

Radhika's joy was evident in her face and heart when she encountered Poonkuzhali and Raghavan at the school. She was thrilled by the unforeseen meeting, and the news they brought only added to her excitement. With enthusiasm and longing, she invited them into her room. She felt immense happiness witnessing the girl, who embraced her suggestion, nearly complete her education and succeed. Radhika viewed Poonkuzhali's success as her personal triumph. It dawned on her that she should do something for Poonkuzhali.

When Radhika began her conversation with Poonkuzhali, Raghavan glanced around her room. It was filled with stacks of books and piles of papers. In the middle of the room, Radhika had placed the Macaw parrot he had given her, safely enclosed in a glass case adorned with flowers. The small table that held only the parrot and the flowers was elegantly and simply adorned, showcasing his gift.

Noticing that Raghavan was staring at the table, Radhika paused her conversation with Poonkuzhali and directed her attention there as well. Diverting his look from the table to Radhika, he silently inquired, "Is this gift so significant?" Radhika grasped the unspoken question in his eyes and nodded "yes," while looking down at the floor. The unseen barrier between them moved slightly. Poonkuzhali observed their unspoken exchange, realizing that the Macaw doll on the table had caught both of their interests.

The commotion was short-lived. Poonkuzhali felt her task was complete. She asked Raghavan, "Shall we leave, uncle?" as she glanced at him. He agreed, saying "OK," and stood up. Radhika quickly held Poonkuzhali's hand, urging her to sit back down. "Just a moment. I'll be right back," she said and exited the room. She returned within five minutes and rejoined them, saying, "Alright, let's go." She had requested time off for the afternoon session at the school.

Despite not comprehending Radhika's behaviour, Raghavan and Poonkuzhali accompanied her without posing any questions. Following that, Radhika led them to a pleasant nearby hotel without seeking their approval. After having lunch, she brought them to a jewellery store. Once inside, she revealed to them that her purpose for visiting the jewellery store was to purchase a gift in recognition of Poonkuzhali's accomplishment.

Raghavan did not mind the situation and left the task of selecting jewellery for Poonkuzhali to the others, casually wandering around the jewellery store as an onlooker. Radhika led Poonkuzhali to the section for golden bangles. Raghavan walked past the rings and approached the area with golden chains, where he also had nothing to do. However, a nearby billboard drew his interest. It showcased a variety of jewels, all of which were antiques. One piece seemed familiar to him. His attention was captured by a pair of anklets displayed there. It appeared to Raghavan that he had seen that piece before, prompting him to move in closer and examine it carefully.

He struggled to recall where he had encountered that locket before, and a slight unease crept over his body. An inch wide anklet crafted with three layers. The first was a strip of silver wire, with the second layer featuring half-inch silver coins suspended from it. The third layer comprised silver beads fastened to the base of each coin. The silver coins and the beads displayed intricate engravings. Each silver coin bore lotus petal designs. Images of raised cobra heads were carved on both sides of the beads. He thought he had seen one of these anklets on the left leg of the Malaimayan. A sudden, startling realization hit him, akin to a lightning strike. One of the clasps attached to the board was missing a silver bead. The line appeared to have tiny symbols damaged or removed from it. The detached silver bead was with Raghavan...!

Overwhelmed with emotions, he stood there in distress. He felt compelled to immediately verify the bead at the house to ensure he wasn't mistaken. He departed from that location and headed to where Poonkuzhali and Radhika were shopping for jewellery. Radhika had given Poonkuzhali a pair of bangles that sparkled on her wrists. Without commenting on this, he escorted Poonkuzhali home, saying goodbye to Radhika while the silver bead lingered in his thoughts.

He eagerly opened the box that held the bead and examined the silver bead inside. Carved into both sides of the bead were distinct figures of cobra heads raised.

Chapter 25

Leopard

After staying for a week, it was time for Poonkuzhali to leave. In the evening, Raghavan stood with her in front of Manikandan's shop. With Chitra away at work, they waited for the bus to the city from the embankment. Poonkuzhali had to go uphill to the town and then make her way solo to the capital city. She had gained the confidence to make the journey. The sound of the bus was audible in the distance. Manikandan emerged from the shop. As the bus came to a stop, Poonkuzhali boarded it with her luggage and waved 'goodbye' to the two people seeing her off. It could be more than a year before she returns after her tests and training.

Manikandan's eyes were filled with concern as he watched the bus vanish from view. He leaned on Raghavan's shoulder for support. Raghavan transformed his child, who might have worked as a daily labourer in a tea mill, into a girl with aspirations for a prestigious job, and this thought weighed heavy on his heart, reflecting in his worried eyes. Raghavan comforted Manikandan, guiding him to sit on the shop bench before joining him. The shop was void of customers, leaving them to sit quietly, each lost in their own thoughts.

Manikandan's mind was occupied with thoughts about Poonkuzhali's marital life. 'While he sustains himself by operating a small roadside shop and his wife works in a tea factory, Poonkuzhali is pursuing a higher position in the government.' He was uncertain about where this would lead. Raghavan did not ponder over Poonkuzhali. She had matured. He was confident she would reach the top soon and trusted that her life would progress accordingly. However, his thoughts were preoccupied with the anklet bead he held. Just then, Uthamaraj's Jeep came to a halt on the paved road in front of the shop, breaking their thoughts.

The person who frequents the dam came from the dam area. The visitor seemed not to have come down for tea. The individual who alighted eagerly instructed those in the vehicle to remain there and hurried to the shop. Upon seeing Raghavan, he joined him, remarking, "Great, you're here too." At Manikandan's shop closing, the man shared shocking news: a leopard had attacked and injured someone working on the cell phone tower installation in Kondarapatti. He mentioned that 'the injured person is being treated at the hospital. He expressed concern that such a hindrance had occurred just days after beginning the tower's construction. The completion deadline for the work was set before the next rainy season. Since then, he had acquired a full-time position in Kondarapatti,' along with additional details.

"A decade ago, a leopard cub was captured in this very village. We safely transported it deep into the forest and released it. Afterwards, there were no issues." Raghavan turned to Uthamaraj, inquiring, "Could that little cheetah have matured and returned?" Uthamaraj responded, "It remains elusive. Typically, animals venture into human settlements in search of food only when they struggle to find it in the wild. If they discover a source of food, they might continue to revisit that location."

"For the last two days, a goat and two chickens have gone missing in Kondarapatti. This might be attributed to the leopard," he mentioned. "It might appear at any moment, so we're planning to establish our camp there," he continued, "let the residents of the Athimedu area know about this. It's a high-traffic zone close to Kondarapatti. I'm informing you to alert you," he expressed with a tone of fear."

Starting the following day, he frequently appeared on the dam road accompanied by four-armed forest guards in his vehicle. Occasionally, he and his team would park the van in front of the shop and conduct patrols in the Athimedu area. However, he mentioned that the leopard was not spotted after that time. Raghavan had also gone to every home in Athimedu to alert people about the leopard and ensured that the doors were secured for safety.

Kondarapatti village was located twelve kilometres away. Manikandan continued to keep his shop open daily, believing that it was unlikely for a leopard to travel such a distance to reach his area. After receiving the information, residents stayed indoors for two days, but eventually, their fear waned, and they resumed their normal activities. Raghavan's fear of the leopard had diminished somewhat. During this period, he also found some work to do.

That morning, a knock echoed on the door of Raghavan's house, leaving the person who answered it in disbelief. The man who had purchased cigarettes from Manikandan's shop months ago was now at the doorstep. On this day, he was without a head-dress and glasses. With a puzzled expression, Raghavan inquired about the situation, to which the newcomer responded that he worked in the tea factory. He stated that the management had sent him with a message: 'Raghavan must visit the management immediately,' and he remained there wearing a mysterious smile.

When Raghavan first encountered the new man at Manikandan's shop, he wasn't impressed. To this day, Raghavan disliked the man's demeanour, the way he delivered information, and how he stood waiting for Raghavan's response with a smile. Raghavan told him, "Alright, let them know I'm on my way." The man at the door nodded, conveying 'as you wish,' without altering his enigmatic smile, then turned and walked toward the tea plant. As Raghavan observed him leave, he noticed something unusual about the man.

While he was walking, he noticed a four-inch gash from the top on the right rear side of his head. He had encountered a similar scar before but couldn't immediately remember where. After some time, he ceased pondering over it and proceeded to the factory for his meeting with the management.

The plant management quickly informed Raghavan of the details. They explained, 'The investigation into Malaimayan's death is complete. It was an accidental death. While alone in the rain, he suffered a leg injury in a minor mishap and passed away after spending an entire night in the rain without anyone to rescue him.' They concluded by telling Raghavan, 'Hunting mansion serves as a memorial for them, and its ongoing upkeep is a tribute to Alan Williams, who founded the tea estate and mill.'

He listened to them intently, nodding his head to indicate understanding, and gazed at them as if urging them to continue. They proceeded to inform Raghavan, "There are challenges in managing the hunting mansion. Due to rumours about the place, no one is willing to work there. However, you are willing. Since the tea plantation's inception, your family has loyally worked at the plantation and the mill. In appreciation, the management is pleased to entrust you with the responsibility of maintaining the hunting mansion at your discretion," they concluded, communicating their decision to Raghavan.

Raghavan did not object to their decision and eagerly anticipated the outcome as he waited. Content with the alignment of events to his expectations, he offered his approval. Following this, they communicated to him, 'You can obtain the mansion key. It is now your duty to safeguard and upkeep it, with maintenance costs to be reimbursed by management.' Afterwards, a conclusive decision from those providing advantageous outcomes left him perplexed and uncertain.

The management communicated all the decisions to Raghavan and eventually mentioned, "We have hired someone to assist you in maintaining the hunting mansion. He is very skilled in maintenance tasks," and then they summoned the assistant. The newcomer, who had been eavesdropping on all their discussions inside up to that point, entered the room and stood before Raghavan, wearing a sarcastic smile.

Despite disagreeing with their final arrangement, Raghavan departed, mentioning he would return to collect the mansion keys the following morning.

Raghavan's mind was unsettled. Throughout his journey home, he was deeply contemplating the hunting mansion. He lost track of time and didn't realize when he arrived. Upon reaching home, he settled on the cement board outside. He neglected to eat lunch. Many different thoughts occupied his mind.

He agreed with the management and departed, knowing he would receive the keys the following day. It all proceeded as he wished. However, a sense of unease bothered him. 'That newcomer...! Why did the management bring him in? They mentioned he was skilled in various maintenance tasks. Was he there to genuinely assist him? Or was he placed by the management to inform them periodically?' Whatever the reason, Raghavan disliked this newcomer. His manner and appearance were very off-putting. His sarcastic behaviour only intensified Raghavan's dislike for him. 'Why did he take on the maintenance?' Raghavan suddenly considered refusing it.

He rejected his fleeting thought. Malaimayan came to his mind. One by one, his creations in the Animal Hall emerged. How splendid they were. They likely started to deteriorate during the time when the mansion was secured. However, the management aims to maintain the hunting mansion as a memorial. His grandfather, Somanathan, had also played a role in building the mansion alongside Malaimayan. He had the impression that they might still be residing with Alan Williams in the mansion. Hence, safeguarding the mansion was crucial.

Although these reflections puzzled him, he felt compelled to continue pondering them. Yet, there was one thing he felt completely certain about.

The metal container holding the clay pieces given to him by Saru as a present was in Malaimayan's residence within the Hunting mansion. It was his belonging, his treasure, and he needed it. To retrieve it, however, he required the keys to the mansion. He contemplated further, thinking, 'Once I have that box, anyone can take care of the mansion.' That box was significant to him; it wasn't merely clay. It represented a living bond.

As he thought of the clay box, his mind drifted to the silver bead and Malaimayan's anklet he noticed in the jeweller's store. It was undoubtedly Malaimayan's belonging. How had it ended up there? Malaimayan only wore the anklet on his left leg, yet in the shop, it was displayed with its pair. Malaimayan may have passed away due to an accident or old age. However, someone might have been present at his passing. Perhaps that person was responsible for Malaimayan's demise. He imagined scenarios where an unidentified person had taken the anklet and its match from Malaimayan's home and sold them to the jeweller.

Raghavan had foreseen the occurrences as though he had witnessed them firsthand. Yet, who was the enigmatic figure? He snickered without leaving evidence. Meanwhile, another detail began to trouble him. The newly arrived individual had a cut mark on the back of his head. How did the image in his mind correspond with the similar scar on the person he recently encountered? How was that feasible? It remained an enigma to Raghavan. Despite his efforts, he couldn't recollect where he had seen the old scenario. His train of thought was suddenly broken by the thrilling events unfolding nearby.

Raghavan rose to his feet upon hearing a group of people sprinting from the vicinity of Manikandan's shop. Uthamaraj and his team were headed towards the tea garden, ignoring Raghavan as they proceeded directly down the incline and into the garden. The expressions and tension on their faces were contagious. Uthamaraj held an unusual gun, with binoculars swinging from his neck. Among his companions, two carried guns, one wielded a machete-like tool, and another had a net. Raghavan followed them and watched as they stood at the mountain slope's edge.

Let by Uthamaraj, his team operated collectively and cohesively, responding to each of his gestures and movements as if they were telepathically connected. Uthamaraj meticulously scanned the whole area from his position using binoculars. Subsequently, the group relocated to a different spot and resumed their search with binoculars.

At that moment, Manikandan emerged from the shop and joined Raghavan. Some of the shop's customers followed and joined him as well. Everyone present was aware of the leopard's movement in Kondarapatti village a few days back, but the reason for their search in the Athimedu area was unclear. The search continued as the team gradually moved down towards the lakeside at the base of the hill. The group, who had been enjoying themselves with Raghavan, lost interest and began to scatter. Raghavan also accompanied Manikandan and sat in the shop. The team's Jeep was parked across the tarred road.

Several hours afterward, Uthamaraj came back with his group, looking exhausted and disheartened. Uthamaraj entered the shop and joined Raghavan at the table. The rest of the group headed directly to the vehicle. Manikandan made tea for all. Uthamaraj appeared troubled and began speaking without waiting for Raghavan to inquire.

In the morning, some individuals claimed to have spotted the leopard near the dam. Prior to the team's arrival, it attacked a worker and then fled. The worker sustained injuries from the leopard's claws. The leopard was not observed in the vicinity after the incident. The search team considered the possibility that it headed towards the tea factory along the leopard's trail. He mentioned there was no chance of going further towards the tea plant. He speculated that the leopard may have returned to the embankment area. He quietly said, 'We won't rest or sleep until we capture it.' Shortly afterwards he and his team moved towards the embankment. Manikandan closed his shop and left, while Raghavan went home and shut the door.

Before retiring for the night, Raghavan resolved that the following morning he would obtain the keys to the hunting mansion. He intended to promptly access Malaimayan's house to retrieve his clay box and return. The decision about the mansion's additional upkeep could be deferred. At that time, he considered not employing an assistant.

Yet whom did destiny abandon? It pursued the newcomer alongside Raghavan. Unforeseen occurrences happened the following day.

Chapter 26

The Trident's Trap

Based on his thoughts the night before, Raghavan completed his tasks early in the morning and headed to the tea factory. He knew exactly what needed to be done. He remembered his plan from the previous night: after obtaining the mansion key, he was to retrieve the clay box from Malaimayan's house and then go back home. However, it was not as straightforward as he had anticipated.

It was after nine in the morning when he exited the house. The valley was blanketed in snow, and the lake below was concealed by it. Raghavan walked by Manikandan's home, stepped into the snow-laden tea garden, and headed towards the tea plant. The cold made his body tremble. Disregarding it, he proceeded past the stone stage platform and into the nearby garden. As he went by the hunting mansion, he saw a group of tea pickers gathered near the mill in the distance, engaged in serious conversation. Raghavan accelerated his steps, suspecting that something unforeseen might have occurred there.

Upon arriving, he realized his suspicions were confirmed. 'Earlier in the day, a leopard attacked a woman while she was harvesting tea in Athimedu. She was transported to the hospital with severe injuries. The forest department has been notified and were enroute. Unable to continue working, everyone gathered at the location,' they mentioned.

Despite finding the information discomforting, he chose to complete the task and depart. As they gave him the mansion's key, the management advised him about the leopard's movements. Raghavan felt relieved that his assigned assistant was absent. He retraced his steps back to the hunting lodge.

After walking a hundred feet, he was halted by an alarm. The blaring siren was succeeded by an announcement through the loudspeaker, alerting Athimedu's residents. A leopard was roaming in the vicinity, prompting a ban on gardening for the day. The forest department was expected to capture the animal by evening, and cooperation from all workers was requested. The vehicle, with sirens blaring, descended and paused briefly at the workers' living area to repeat the announcement.

Moments after the announcement, Uthamaraj's vehicle sped to the location, his team disembarking in front of Manikandan's store. Armed with the same weapons as the day before, they carefully navigated the Athimedu slope into the tea fields. With guns and weapons at the ready, they spread into a line, descending with caution in a methodical 'combing operation' approach. Positioned centrally, Uthamaraj carried a tranquilizer gun capable of rendering animals unconscious by delivering anaesthesia from afar.

Despite the warning, Raghavan remained resolute and departed from the tea factory, proceeding onto the path toward the hunting mansion.

Simultaneously, the factory assistant received word that Raghavan was heading to the hunting mansion with the key. Having awaited the mansion's opening for a considerable period, he resolved to execute his plan that day and hastened to the mansion.

Uthamaraj's team had arrived at the base of the hill. After ensuring there was no leopard in the vicinity, they chose the next section of the hill's slope and began their search from the bottom going upwards. Their search area concluded at the stone stage area at the summit.

Raghavan arrived at the rear of the hunting mansion and proceeded towards the side of Malaimayan's house, unaware that the assistant trailed behind him.

The person trailing Raghavan observed from afar that Raghavan had moved towards the rear of the mansion and then headed in the direction of Malaimayan's home. Carefully, he advanced towards the back of the mansion and observed Raghavan, concealed behind a tree.

The individuals who began their journey from the base of the hills were looking for the garden's centre at that moment. They did not encounter any surprises in the garden. However, one awaited them at the conclusion of the search zone, on the stone platform.

Raghavan headed directly to Malaimayan's house, opened the door, and went inside. The box he was seeking wasn't present in the living room. Frustrated, Raghavan hurried into the kitchen and looked all over but couldn't find the box.

The individual concealed behind the tree at the rear of the mansion felt thrilled upon hearing dishes clattering and rolling within Malaimayan's residence. It was clear that the disabled man was looking for something inside. He also started to scrutinize the area closely.

The group on the lookout approached the stone platform. Fifty more feet, and the tea plantation came to an end, giving way to the stone stage area with its bushes and undergrowth. Resting beneath the peepal tree was the leopard they sought, appearing somewhat weary due to a lack of adequate nourishment over the last week.

Disappointed, Raghavan stood in Malaimayan's house, convinced that if the box wasn't present there, it must be inside the mansion. He promptly went to the mansion, opened its doors, and went inside.

After observing Raghavan depart from Malaimayan's house and enter the mansion, the assistant quietly emerged from behind the tree and approached the door of Malaimayan's house. Slightly concealed, he peeked into the mansion through the window. Inside, he noticed the man hobbling toward the animal hall.

When the group was ten feet away from the stone stage, the man positioned second to the right of Uthamaraj spotted the leopard and quickly alerted the team. Instantly, everyone crouched down to the level of the tea plants and cautiously moved forward. The bushes near the stone stage provided them with cover. Uthamaraj inspected his dart gun. Unfortunately, the leopard noticed the individual to Uthamaraj's left as they entered the bushy area around the stone stage. In a split second, it leaped and attacked him fiercely. The chaos was immediate as the leopard jumped onto him and began biting viciously. His screams made the others wince. Uthamaraj, who was nearby, promptly prepared to shoot the leopard. Upon hearing the commotion, the leopard turned its head, swiftly rose from the man on the ground, and lunged at Uthamaraj.

Uthamaraj, poised to fire, encountered a sudden attack as the leopard lunged at him, causing him to instinctively pull the trigger. The anaesthetic dart from the gun grazed the leopard's moving front paw and fell elsewhere. The leopard toppled onto him, forcing him to duck at the same moment he shot it. It got back on its feet and staggered, then upon noticing approaching people, swiftly retreated through the tea bushes.

The people gathered there helped the man who had fallen and began to care for him. Uthamaraj understood that it was unpredictable how an animal might behave after being injured. He entrusted the injured man to another person for assistance and proceeded to track the leopard with the other two guards. The leopard, not having gone far, was faltering among the tea plants a short way off. The leopard wobbled, unable to move steadily as if the anaesthetic arrow from the gun had injected some sedative into its system. Upon observing the leopard's movement, Uthamaraj felt a sense of hope and began to trace the leopard's path with two others at a prudent distance.

While searching for the clay box in the animal hall, Raghavan quickly found it near a heap of clay in the left corner. As he stooped to retrieve it, he noticed another box.

The corner of this box jutted out slightly from a stack of animal skins lying beside the dirt pile. With anticipation, Raghavan drew the box from its hiding place among the skins. It was also a small box that could be held between two hands. Curious, he opened it.

Inside the box were various glass fragments of assorted sizes. Among them were also the nails and teeth of animals. Malaimayan had gathered these items for the purpose of crafting animal exhibits using the 'Taxidermy' technique. As Raghavan ran his fingers over the materials, he was taken aback by a solitary red stone mingled with the glass fragments. A notion struck him suddenly. 'Could it be?' He recalled that Malaimayan had recounted past incidents when he had hastily combined it with the glass beads in a container. That invaluable gem had been in that box all these years. He was in disbelief.

With his left hand, he grabbed the stone, set the box atop the clay pile, and held the stone up to his eyes, gazing through the window. He couldn't discern anything about it. Exiting the animal hall, he descended to the floor of the reception room, which was a step below. As he stood there, he noticed the goddess statue directly overhead. He was meant to align the stone in his hand with the goddess's crown. Clutching the stone between his left thumb and forefinger, he placed it right before his eyes at the indentation where it fit into the crown visible above.

He felt it was a perfect match. Turning once more towards the door, he noticed it illuminated by the light from the room's left window. The window's light shone through the stone, casting a reddish glow on his face. He pondered the years, the troubles, the losses...! He considered it a stroke of luck, gazing at it in his hand. He didn't realize that misfortune also kept following him.

To the thief observing Raghavan from the right-side window, it appeared like a sudden stroke of luck. As he saw Raghavan in the reception room with a red stone in his hand, a flurry of thoughts filled his mind. How long had he been waiting for this moment? The red glow from the stone on Raghavan's face clouded his consciousness and filled him with excitement. He hurried to the mansion's door, eager to take it right away.

In a slight daze, the cheetah staggered towards the hunting lodge, paying no attention to the trio trailing behind it. Uthamaraj and his companions, who were at the rear, tracked the leopard by moving to wherever it veered, concealing themselves within the foliage and forest. Uthamaraj meticulously tailed the leopard, biding his time for the ideal opportunity with the second anaesthetic dart in his firearm. He still had a single dart remaining.

Raghavan was positioned directly beneath the statue of Amman with his crutch, observing the red stone in his left hand. A movement at the mansion's entrance caught his attention, prompting him to glance towards it. He noticed his assistant approaching. Detecting the erratic behaviour in his walk and expression jolted Raghavan into alertness. Quickly, Raghavan stood upright, facing him with a mix of urgency and determination. The thief swiftly approached and stopped three feet away from Raghavan.

His eyes lingered hungrily on the red gem held in Raghavan's left hand. Next, he glanced at Raghavan's crutch with a carefree attitude and mocked him with a harsh laugh. Noticing the direction of his gaze, Raghavan discerned the ideas forming in his mind. Quickly, he slipped the red stone into his pants pocket, discarded the crutch from his right hand, tightened his fists, and readied himself to confront him.

Raghavan's behaviour infuriated him even further. The situation mirrored the past when his father had placed the diamond in his pocket, only to have it taken away in the same room a decade ago. This memory ignited an intense anger within him. Observing Raghavan's limp and his readiness to engage in combat, his fury escalated, prompting him to abruptly move forward and kick Raghavan in the chest.

Raghavan, remaining vigilant, foresaw the move and used his left hand to intercept and redirect the incoming leg, while simultaneously delivering a powerful punch to his opponent's face with his right hand. Raghavan's punch shattered his front teeth, ripped his lips, and blood poured from his mouth. He was propelled in reverse and tumbled. At the same time, Raghavan also fell backwards due to the impact of his punch. Raghavan's head hit the edge of the platform leading to the animal hall, which had risen somewhat from the reception room floor, knocking him unconscious. After a few seconds, the thief woke up and crawled near Raghavan, wiping the blood from his mouth. Seeing that Raghavan was unconscious, he hurriedly took the red stone from his pocket.

As he retrieved the red stone from his pocket, the distressed leopard entered the mansion. It failed to notice someone lying on the floor below the goddess statue and another person kneeling beside it. Desperately seeking refuge, and with its mind fogged by mild anaesthesia, it stumbled up the stairs on the left to the upstairs veranda. It moved to the veranda's opposite side because Alan Williams's room was shut, observed the descending steps, and retraced its path.

Uthamaraj, carrying his arrow gun, trailed the injured leopard to the mansion's entrance and quickly spotted it roaming the first floor. Without hesitation, he entered, lifting his weapon to target the leopard above, completely oblivious to the two people on the ground level.

As Uthamaraj aimed his firearm at the leopard, it returned from the opposite end of the veranda, positioned itself behind the Amman statue on the terrace's edge, and placed its forelegs on the statue, peering down while tilting its head to the right of the deity's head. At that moment, a dart fired from Uthamaraj's readied weapon. His aim was accurate, but he overlooked the Trident, which was held by the goddess between the panther's head and himself.

With the red stone in his grasp, the thief, filled with anger, perched on Raghavan's chest, and began choking him, ominously saying, "join your father...!" Meanwhile...

The dart, cutting through the air, hit the middle of the Trident held by the Goddess with a quick 'ding' noise and splattered.

Earlier, the thief aiming to steal the diamond had climbed onto the statue and placed his foot on the wrist that held the Trident, compromising its stability. Subsequently, the right wrist of the Amman statue, already weakened over the years by temperature changes, broke away from the hand and fell along with the Trident. The Trident's tip, once detached from the goddess's hand, aimed straight for the thief's head, who was attempting to harm Raghavan on the ground below.

Resolving to choke Raghavan and send him to his father, he began to squeeze his neck and looked up upon hearing a sound over his head. In an instant, the Trident, positioned to strike his head, instead went directly through his chest. The Trident descended with force, striking his chest, tearing his heart, and taking his life instantly. His inert form fell backwards to the earth. His hands, lifted high above his head, descended at the same speed, and struck the room's floor with a 'thud', 'thud' sound. During the impact, the red stone he grasped in his right hand slipped out, quickly rolled, and crashed into the mansion's wall, breaking into tiny glass shards...!

After the second arrow missed its target, Uthamaraj rose with the one last arrow left in his firearm. The panther, which was behind the statue of the goddess, was alarmed by the sound of the arrow striking the Trident and descended the stairs. Uthamaraj acted. This time he hit the target. The arrow struck the leopard's forehead directly. In the following moment, the leopard fell on the stairs. The two individuals accompanying Uthamaraj hurried to the stairs, carrying a net in their hands.

Raghavan rose, clutching the back of his head, and sat down extending his legs. Before him lay the newcomer who intended to murder him, upright with a Trident embedded in his chest, deceased. He was clueless about the events that transpired.

Uthamaraj knelt, placing the gun's butt on the ground to ease himself after moving the leopard. It was then that he noticed what had happened. On the same floor, Raghavan was seated with his legs extended, and a lifeless body lay before him. In a sudden state of panic, Uthamaraj stood up and hurried over to Raghavan.

Chapter 27

Blessing of the Fig Tree

Residents of Athimedu continued to discuss the awful occurrences that transpired at the hunting mansion. Though more than ten days had passed since the event, discussions were still ongoing. Raghavan and Uthamaraj became quite popular both in their community and the neighbouring town, with Uthamaraj being celebrated as a hero.

Although the episodes at the hunting lodge under their oversight surprised the tea estate management, no one was held responsible for what happened. Additionally, the recent deceased was a convicted murderer. After being informed by the police that he was a prisoner, he was not discussed further.

Tales of paranormal activities around the hunting mansion were circulating. In this situation, the management of the tea plantation was confused about maintaining the mansion. Once again, they turned to Raghavan for assistance. He was tasked with managing the upkeep of both the mansion and the animal specimens inside until the administration decided. Raghavan happily accepted their request.

A few days each week, he habitually visited the hunting mansion to carry out maintenance. He meticulously searched every corner of the mansion, driven by a lingering quest in his mind. There was nothing left to examine; he couldn't locate the red diamond. It dawned on him that what he found that day in the mansion was merely a piece of glass, shattering to reveal its true nature. The diamond's secret was laid to rest with Malaimayan, the sole person who was privy to its existence. Having never seen it with his own eyes, he eventually forgot about it. His primary focus turned to the mansion's artefacts, and a path for this was also established through Poonkuzhali.

Poonkuzhali had successfully passed the personality test following her achievement in the main examination and was currently at a training camp in the northern region of the country. Except for when Raghavan visited the hunting estate, he would frequently engage in conversations with Manikandan at the shop. Consequently, the seasons progressed, with the rainy season commencing and concluding. The following rainy season was once again on the horizon.

That morning, after Raghavan departed for the hunting lodge, he completed his tasks and headed directly to Manikandan's shop, where he took a seat. At noon, a taxi arrived, pulling to a gentle stop in front of Manikandan's store. Raghavan and Manikandan watched attentively to see who would step out. Poonkuzhali emerged from the vehicle shortly after. Both faces lit up with delight at the unexpected appearance of Poonkuzhali, who arrived without prior notification. Raghavan rose to greet her, while Manikandan descended from the shop to assist her with her luggage.

After setting aside her belongings and reversing the car, Poonkuzhali walked directly towards Raghavan with an unwavering and direct gaze. Upon reaching him, she bowed down, touched his feet with both hands, and met his eyes. She then stood up and swiftly saluted Raghavan with respect. Raghavan acknowledged her without comprehending the situation. "Uncle, I have become a collector, just as you wished," she announced proudly, keeping her hand raised in a salute.

Unsure of how to react to the joyous news, he smiled and said, "I anticipated you would arrive like this someday." Poonkuzhali shifted to Raghavan's right side and laid her head on his shoulder. Manikandan, who had collected and organized her belongings, stood leaning on Raghavan's left shoulder. They all appreciated the moment. Raghavan appeared distressed, with tears streaming down his face.

After sending her home with Manikandan, and promising to meet at home in the evening, he went back. In the evening Raghavan visited Manikandan's house, Chitra and Poonkuzhali were busy cooking indoors. Raghavan settled on the doorstep. Poonkuzhali served him a bowl of hot cassava tubers, then fetched another bowl for herself and joined him on the step. Manikandan, arriving after closing the shop, also sat on the steps, and Chitra brought him a bowl and joined them as well.

Fifteen years earlier, the same quartet sat in the identical spot. On that occasion too, they held hot boiled cassava in their hands. Raghavan reflected on the contrast between the circumstances of the past and those of the present. As they ate, the three of them listened to Poonkuzhali share the specifics.

Poonkuzhali recapped the occurrences of the past year and mentioned that she secured a position with the Government of India. She went indoors, retrieved the appointment letter, and showed Raghavan that she had been assigned to work in the northern state. She then informed them that she would need to report for duty in two weeks to accept her role. Chitra and Manikandan didn't fully grasp Poonkuzhali's accomplishment. However, Chitra was thrilled about her daughter's attainment of a prestigious government role, while Manikandan did not display any joy. Raghavan knew that Poonkuzhali's advancement was no trivial matter, but rather an impressive achievement. He warmly congratulated Poonkuzhali and requested a favour from her. Raghavan asked her to visit him the following day so he could explain his request to her then.

The following day, after Chitra had left for the factory, Poonkuzhali arrived early at Raghavan's house. Raghavan was seated in the first room, anticipating her visit. Poonkuzhali took a seat on the floor before him and inquired, "Tell me, uncle, what should I do." Raghavan appreciated Poonkuzhali for becoming a powerful government official and wrapped up by detailing the incidents at the hunting mansion, deliberately omitting any reference to the red diamond. He posed the question of what to do with the invaluable animal figurines crafted by Malaimayan in the hunting mansion, as only he ventured into that place. He earnestly sought her guidance and help in the matter.

To his astonishment, Poonkuzhali disclosed her idea immediately. She also shared her opinion about the goddess statue in the hunting mansion. Moreover, she assured that if he approved her idea, she would approach the government officials to obtain permission for its execution. Raghavan found her ideas to be highly appropriate and pertinent. After agreeing to her plan, he inquired about Manikandan and Chitra, expressing his interest in knowing her thoughts about her parents.

She promptly told him about the decision she had already made. Her choice was beneficial for them. While moving to her workplace, both her mother and father would accompany her. Raghavan was pleased with her choice as it meant they wouldn't have to endure hardships here anymore.

They quickly set to work implementing their plan regarding the hunting mansion. After notifying Manikandan that they intended to meet with some government officials, the pair hurried to the city on his motorbike. Following that, they spent the days continuously doing the same tasks. Over the week, they arranged meetings with the necessary government officials and, with their approval, also met with the tea mill management to secure their agreement and support. In two days, after obtaining government authorization for the project, they scheduled the execution date and began their efforts.

Both agreed that Friday was the most suitable day of the week. Poonkuzhali planned to accompany her family on

Saturday after fulfilling their agenda on Friday. The tea estate management covered the costs and made all the arrangements for everything related to the hunting mansion. The tasks were completed very swiftly. On Friday morning, the area of Athimedu was bustling as if it were a minor festival. People were all congregated in the stone stage area. Under Poonkuzhali's supervision, the stone stage platform was converted into a small temple. The surrounding bushes were entirely cleared, and flowering plants and trees were planted in their place. The stone stage was restored and provided with a roof. Poonkuzhali brought the statue of Amman from the hunting mansion and sanctified it on the stone stage. The Trident, which had been separated from Amman's hand, was also properly affixed to the idol. The idol of Amman was presented in the same state as it was when Raghavan's grandfather Somanathan and Malaimayan first observed it.

As the goddess statue was being placed on the stone platform and the religious rituals were underway, the animal exhibits from the hunting lodge were being removed, individually boxed, and loaded onto a truck. They have all been donated to the Government Museum. The authorities chose to clear out the hunting mansion and transform the building into a tea plant management office to honour Alan Williams. All was proceeding according to Poonkuzhali's guidance.

Raghavan, positioned in front of the stone stage and joyfully observing the events, was also watching the mansion being evacuated in the mansion vicinity. Suddenly, an idea struck his mind with the speed of lightning. 'Could it be true?' His thoughts turned frantic, and his body started to tremble. 'What ignorance! How did something so obvious slip past him unnoticed?' Without delay, he hurried to the hunting mansion to verify the idea that had occurred to him.

When he arrived at the hunting lodge, the final box was prepared for loading onto the truck. Raghavan quickly approached the box and asked about its contents. The people there mentioned, "There is a black panther model." Feeling reassured that it matched his expectations, he moved closer to inspect the box through the gap in the boards.

In the dim light within the box, the black panther toy gazed with its fiery eyes. Then, a beam of light from an unknown source hit the doll's eyes and penetrated Raghavan's vision, brightening his mind. At that instant, Poonkuzhali rang the bell mounted on the stone platform before the Goddess statue. As the temple bells echoed 'ding... ding... ding...,' Raghavan felt enlightened, and his mind was at ease. They placed the final box into the truck in front of Raghavan. The truck moved gradually, drawing Raghavan's attention to the government seal on the last box marked 'Government Property.'

Raghavan and Poonkuzhali were delighted that everything went according to plan. The following morning, Poonkuzhali, as she had decided, took Chitra and Manikandan to the hill town. That evening, they all departed from there heading north.

The information Manikandan shared with Raghavan before departing was troubling him. The story was regarding Radhika teacher. Manikandan explained, "Radhika Teacher faced misfortune; she lost her spouse just one month after getting married. Her husband, Senthilkumar, was killed in a bomb explosion while on military duty," and added, "Poonkuzhali wanted me to inform you," before he left.

Why did Poonkuzhali direct Manikandan to relay that information to him? While pondering this, Raghavan was unexpectedly visited by Saru, who fluttered in from the backyard and landed on his shoulder. It had been a long time since Saru's last visit. Intriguingly, another parrot trailed Saru, perching at the backyard entrance and calling out 'kee… kee….' Saru on Raghavan's shoulder echoed with its own 'kee… kee…' before taking flight to join its companion. Raghavan rose from the front room and proceeded to the backyard. As he approached, the two parrots took to the fig tree. To observe them, Raghavan went out to the lawn and stood beneath the tree. He noted that Saru's demeanour was unusual that day. The parrots, nestled together on a branch, continued their 'kee… kee… kee… kee…' cries, affectionately nudging each other. Despite his attempts, Saru did not respond to his calls. Raghavan struggled to decipher the message they seemed to carry, lamenting his inability to speak the parrots' language.

Among the group conversing with him in the parrot's language for some time, Saru's companion suddenly took flight, and subsequently, Saru followed and reunited with its partner. To Raghavan, they appeared to be dancing and singing in the heavens. As was typical, Raghavan observed until Saru vanished from sight, and he somehow sensed that Saru would not return.

In the evening, Raghavan sat by himself outside Manikandan's locked shop, which he owned. Following their discussion, where Manikandan initially declined to accompany Poonkuzhali the day before, he only agreed to go after Raghavan promised to manage the shop in his absence.

While sitting at the entrance of the closed shop, reflecting on his predicament, he realized everyone who had been around him had departed. Father and Malaimayan had left him permanently. Poonkuzhali, Chitra, and Manikandan, who once supported him, had gone their separate ways. Finally, even Saru took flight with its mate. A sense of emptiness filled his mind. His thoughts drifted aimlessly like a vine caught in the wind, lacking a branch to hold onto. At that moment, a car quietly pulled up in front of the shop.

The person who absentmindedly expected company at the closed shop was in for a surprise. Radhika arrived to visit him, disembarking from her car. In his rush to stand, Raghavan's crutch slipped and fell. Radhika reached him before he could retrieve it, bent down, and picked it up. Instead of handing it back, she bravely opted to hold onto it. With the crutch in her right hand, she stepped to his side, taking his right hand and placing it on her left shoulder, as if silently declaring, 'I will be your crutch from now on.'

The car's window, parked on the asphalt road, was rolled down, and Poonkuzhali, smilingly waved at them and bid farewell, content with having united them.

At the break of dawn, Raghavan and Radhika stood beneath the fig tree. The sky lightened to a pale white as the light diffused. Moments later, the sun emerged, bathing the entire area in sunlight. With a soft breeze, the fig tree swayed and dropped its leaves, bestowing blessings upon the couple beneath.

The new beginning!